"Ride!" Nate said, and ground. The Leonards in despite their inexperience.

To the northwest rose fe Bloods realized their quarry had outfoxed them.

"They're after us!" Elden cried. "We're doomed."

"Quiet, damn you!" Nate said over his shoulder. Out of the corner of his eye he spied what appeared to be a break in the trees, and he guided the stallion into it. Too late he saw that the break was actually a small half-moon clearing that bordered a high hill.

"What do we do?" Elden yelled.

About to gallop along the base of the hill, Nate spotted braves directly in front of him. As he went to snap off a shot, a whizzing arrow appeared as a pale blur coming straight at his head . . . .

BLOOD TRUCE

Nate started to step backward and aim the Hawken at the phantom figure, but his adversary was on him before he could squeeze the trigger. A heavy body slammed into his chest, knocking the wind out of him even as he was brutally smashed to the earth.

As Nate made a valiant effort to stand and resist the attackers, rough hands tore the Hawken from his hands. Other men seized his arms and held them fast while his pistols, knife, and tomahawk were stripped from him.

At the corner of the cabin a similar struggle was taking place. Zach was in the grip of three buckskin-clad Indians, who had taken his rifle and were trying to wrest his knife from him.

From inside the cabin, Winona shouted, "What has happened? Are you all right?"

"Stay in there and keep the door barred!" Nate said. "The Utes have us!"

WILDERNESS

WINTERKILL/
BLOOD TRUCE

David Thompson

LEISURE BOOKS   NEW YORK CITY

A LEISURE BOOK®

February 1999

Published by

Dorchester Publishing Co., Inc.
276 Fifth Avenue
New York, NY 10001

ISBN 0-8439-4489-7

WINTERKILL

To Judy, Joshua, and Shane.

Chapter One

The regal Rocky Mountains were cloaked in a thick mantle of gleaming snow. Every boulder, every tree, was covered by the white blanket. From out of the northwest blew a gusty wind that stirred the surface of this pristine natural wonderland, creating swirling sprays of fine white mist. Other than the subdued whispering of the wind and the rustling of the whipping snow, there was no sound. Gone were the scampering chipmunks and chattering squirrels, the chirping birds and the yipping coyotes. The animals knew better than to be abroad when winter had the Rockies in its fierce icy grip.

Nate King also knew better, but he had no choice. He was a free trapper by trade, and he lived in a remote corner of the vast mountains with his Shoshone wife, Winona, his young son, Zach, and his infant daughter, Evelyn. Because of them he was braving the cold and the formidable terrain in search of large game; their supply of food was critically low. Unless he brought back fresh meat soon, they would be in dire straits before another week went by.

Buckskins covered Nate's muscular form. A beaver hat and a heavy buffalo robe insulated him from the worst of the biting chill. Moccasins, wrapped round with strips from an old blanket, protected his feet.

Nate idly reached up and scratched his thick beard, which he always allowed to grow longer and thicker during the colder months. Below him stretched a meandering valley. The only sign of movement was in the sluggish stream that cut the valley floor into two halves. If there were black-tailed deer or elk down below, they were keeping well hidden.

Moving with extreme care, Nate descended the slope he had been traversing, the reins held firmly in his right hand. Clasped in the crook of his left elbow was his trusty Hawken. Under his robe, lodged under his wide brown leather belt, were two flintlock pistols. On his right hip rested a tomahawk, on his left a large butcher knife. A powder horn, an ammo pouch, and a possibles bag completed the inventory of articles he usually carried on his person. The rest of his meager provisions were stored in the twin parfleches that hung over the back of his sturdy black stallion, right behind the saddle.

Nate was two days out from his cabin, to the north of his ordinary haunts. He knew there were many secluded valleys to be found here, and in one of them he hoped to bag the meat his family needed. Consequently, as he neared the base of the mountain, he worked his fingers back and forth inside the bulky fur mittens covering them to insure his hands would be warm and limber when it came time to use his rifle.

The almost total lack of noise proved unsettling. Nate was accustomed to the myriad calls and cries of the abundant wildlife, to the constant sighing of the trees and the grass. The absence of familiar sounds lent the sea of snow an alien aspect. Underneath, locked in frozen slumber, was the vibrant land he loved so much, the land that had claimed his soul just as the lovely Winona had claimed his heart.

Although no one would know it to look at him, Nate King was New York born and bred. A product of the bustling city, he had learned to cherish the savage wilderness. He had also done what few other white men had been able to accomplish; he had adapted to the harsh demands of life in the Rockies as superbly as the Indians whose ways he so admired.

Grizzly Killer was the name the Indians called him, courtesy of a noted Cheyenne warrior who had once seen him slay a huge silver-tip with just a knife. Few men, white or Indian, could boast of such a feat. So now the friendly tribes, the Shoshones, Flatheads, Nez Perce, and the Crows, all knew him by that name, as did the hostile tribes, those devoted to the extermination of all whites, namely the Blackfeet, the Piegans, the Utes, and others.

Nate reached the valley floor and made toward the stream. The stallion's hoofs clumped dully in the deep snow and its breath formed small puffy clouds in the crisp air. His own breath did likewise, and occasionally, if he carelessly left his lips parted for too long, it felt as if his mouth had been frozen solid. He had to repeatedly open and close it and rub his lips with his mittens to restore sensation.

A low gurgling came from the gently bubbling stream. Only the water in the center flowed freely. Along both borders hung strips of ice that would gradually widen with each passing day. Eventually, the stream would become covered with a thick sheet if a spell of warm weather didn't provide relief from the frigid arctic weather first.

Nate moved along the west bank, his keen green eyes roving over both sides, seeking sign that deer or elk had come to drink. Once he found fresh tracks, he would follow them, and with a little luck he'd have the meat he needed before nightfall.

Half a mile into the valley, as Nate drew abreast of a thick stand of pines, he spotted a disturbed area in the snow ahead. Jabbing his heels into the stallion's flanks, he trotted closer, then reined up in consternation.

The snow had been torn up by the passage of a dozen horses that had emerged from the pines, stopped at the stream to drink, and then turned up the valley, heading for the far end. Two of the horses, as the hoofprints clearly indicated, had been shod; the rest had not.

Nate scanned the gleaming expanse of snow but saw no sign of the large party. His mind was racing as he pondered the implications. Since there were no other free trappers living in the region, and the company men were all down in the low country wintering over at Fort Laramie, the tracks must have been made by Indians. Yet if so, Nate mused, what were two white men doing in the party, as the shod hoofs showed was the case? Were they trappers who preferred to live with Indians? That was possible but unlikely since few of the trappers bothered to have their horses shod. They rode unshod mounts, Indian fashion.

Moving on, Nate studied the trail. Another possibility occurred to him and made him grip the Hawken a little tighter. There was a chance the band was composed of hostiles, and they might have stolen the two shod horses from white men they'd slain. Should they spot him, he'd be in danger of suffering the same fate. But Nate pressed on anyway. If he had any common sense, he wryly told himself, he'd go elsewhere and leave the mysterious riders to mind their own affairs. His curiosity, though, wouldn't let him. He had to find out who these riders were and what they were doing in that particular area.

The tracks wound into high hills beyond the valley. Here Nate slowed, every nerve tingling, alert to the slightest sounds and vaguest smells. The hills were heavily forested, many of the trees stooped under the heavy weight of the snow. West of them reared a towering peak. All appeared tranquil, yet Nate knew how deceptive appearance could be.

It was the stallion that forewarned him. They were skirting the base of a hill dotted with massive boulders when the horse jerked its head up, nostrils flaring. Nate sniffed loudly, testing the wind. Seconds later he detected the faint, acrid scent of wood smoke. He stopped and dismounted, then tied the reins to the branch of a handy evergreen and advanced up a short incline. At the rim he hunkered down to peer over.

The band had camped in a sheltered nook several hundred yards away. Flanked by sheer slopes on two sides, it afforded excellent protection from the wind. Nate could see the 12 horses tied in a row to the north of the fire. Bustling about were a number of warriors, while others huddled near the dancing flames. The Indians were too far off for him to identify so, moving into the trees to his right, Nate crept closer.

Soon voices and laughter could be heard. The warriors were relaxed, no doubt feeling secure in their sheltered hideaway, which worked in Nate's favor. They wouldn't be as vigilant as usual, enabling him to get close without being seen.

The snow also helped immensely. Nate's measured footfalls were totally silent, and the many drifts offered plenty of concealment. His main worry was inadvertently exposing himself for even a few seconds since his dark robe would stand out in stark contrast to the surrounding background of shimmering white. Overhead the sun blazed, yet the day might as well have been overcast for all the warming effect it had.

By exercising stealth an Apache would have envied, Nate drew within 15 yards of the encampment. Lying on his stomach behind a mound of snow, he removed his beaver hat and warily eased his head out far enough to see what was going on. The Indians, he now realized, were Bloods, staunch allies of the dreaded Blackfeet. He counted ten braves all tolled, and wondered where the last two might be. Then he heard a new voice raised in anger.

"Give us something to eat and drink, for God's sake! It's been two days now!"

Startled, Nate glanced to the north and was shocked to see a pair of people lying bound on the exposed ground, two whites, no less, and *one of them was a woman!* He gaped, not because of the color of their skin, but because they wore clothes typical of those who lived in cities and towns back in the States. The woman had on a dress under an ankle-length coat, the man a suit and a coat sporting a fur collar. None of their garments were practical for wilderness travel. The two were as out of place there as a grizzly would have been strolling the streets of New York City or Philadelphia.

A score of questions filtered through Nate's mind: Who were they? What were they doing in the mountains in the dead of winter? How had they managed to get themselves caught by the Bloods?

Nate saw a burly warrior stand and walk from the fire to the captives. The brave barked angry words in the Blood tongue, then hauled off and kicked the male captive in the ribs, doubling the man over in agony.

"Leave him alone!" the woman screamed defiantly. "Why must you insist on tormenting us so? We've done nothing to you."

The warrior stepped to her side and raised a hand as if to slap her. Instead of cringing in fear, the woman held her head higher and met his glare with one of her own. After several seconds the Blood merely grunted, lowered his arm, and returned to the fire.

Nate, taking his hat in his left hand, worked his way northward. He wasn't quite sure what he could do to help the pair, but he must do something. The Bloods were probably heading to their village. Once there, the white woman would be taken in by one of the warriors and forced to be his wife whether she liked the notion or not. The man faced a worse end; he'd be tortured until he died, made to endure a horrible, lingering death.

A log piled high with snow lay near the captives. Behind this Nate halted to listen.

"Elden? Elden? How bad is it?" the woman was asking.

"The damn devil nearly broke my ribs," responded the man hoarsely. "My stomach is queasy too. I fear I might be sick at any minute."

"I'd like to get my hands on a pistol! I'd teach these red barbarians not to abuse us!"

"Don't do anything else to antagonize them, Selena. You can see how they are."

"Are we supposed to give up hope then? Let them have their dirty way with us?" Selena muttered something under her breath, concluding with, "I'll be damned if I'll give up without a fight! With my dying breath I'll resist them if need be."

Nate found himself admiring the woman's gumption. He risked lifting his head high enough to peek over the log. Thankfully, none of the warriors were paying the least bit attention to the captives. Some were collecting wood, others were intent on one of their number who was skinning a rabbit. Nate glanced at the captives, taking their measure.

Up close, the woman was quite attractive. Shoulder-length brown hair framed an oval face distinguished by full rosy lips and sparkling blue eyes. The man had black hair and lackluster dark eyes. His face was tinged by a hint of corpulence, his chin fleshy and bulging, and his suit swelled around the waist.

"I've been working on these cords," Elden now commented, "but it's useless. If only I could get to my knife."

Nate saw that their arms had been bent behind them and their wrists lashed to their ankles with cord made from buckskin. He thought of slipping them his knife, but suddenly a warrior by the fire stood, so Nate dropped below the log again. Soft footsteps came nearer. Then the warrior spoke gruffly and there was an odd sort of sound, a muffled plop, followed by hearty laughter as the Blood moved off.

"He can't mean what I think he means," Elden said forlornly.

"You wanted something to eat. Help yourself."

Propping his elbows under him, Nate took a quick look-see. Lying in a small pile beside Elden was the rabbit's bloody hide, its four severed feet, and several raw strips of stringy flesh. Since it was doubtful any of the Bloods understood English, he figured the warriors must have guessed why Elden had been squawking and shown their contempt for his display of weakness in this manner. Elden now had his thick lips scrunched up distastefully, while Selena was staring at the pile in simmering indignation. She abruptly looked up, straight at the log, and her mouth went slack in astonishment. Instantly Nate flattened, fearing she would cry out and give his presence away. But there was only silence for perhaps ten seconds. Then Elden spoke.

"Are you all right?"

"Yes," Selena mumbled. "Why?"

"You had the most peculiar look there for a few moments, as if you were the one who was going to be violently ill, not I. Try eating some snow. It might help settle your stomach."

"What do we do?"

"I don't understand. Do in relation to what?" Elden sighed. "There's nothing we can do unless we get free, and we can't do that with these damn savages watching us like hawks all the time."

"I wasn't talking to you," Selena said softly.

"What? Then who?"

"The man behind the log."

Nate heard the sound of someone moving.

"Don't turn, you dunderhead!" Selena said. "Do you want the Indians to know someone is out there?"

"But—" Elden began excitedly.

"Don't talk. Just lie there and act as if nothing is happening," Selena advised. Her voice acquired an insistent tone, and Nate knew she was addressing him. "I'll ask you again, sir. What do we do? I saw part of your beard, so I know you're white, like us. Surely you'll help us escape from these fiends, won't you?"

Nate edged to the end of the log and cupped a hand to his mouth. "I'll be back after dark," he whispered. "Be ready."

There was a gasp, apparently from Elden. "I thought you were imagining things, Selena!" He paused. "Who are you, mister? Are you alone? Please save us. *Please*.

I don't think I can take much more of this brutal treatment. I—"

"Stop blubbering," Selena said sharply. "Bite your lip if you have to, but keep your mouth shut. We mustn' do anything to attract those Indians over here."

"Sorry," Elden responded meekly.

Nate saw no reason to stay and increase the odds of being discovered. He backed away from the log until he was hidden in the trees; then he rose into a crouch, donned his hat, and retraced his steps to the stallion. He was greatly impressed by the woman's courage and self-control and how quickly she reacted to a crisis. The man, on the other hand, gave every evidence of being one of those pampered, prissy Easterners who couldn't survive unaided in the wild if their lives depended on it, which often was the case once they foolishly ventured west of the Mississippi River.

Reaching his horse, Nate climbed up and moved into the sanctuary of the forest. Some of the Bloods might leave the camp to hunt more game and he didn't want them stumbling on him before the time came to free Selena and Elden. He found a secluded small clearing hemmed in by trees, and there he kicked enough snow aside to allow the stallion to get at the brown grass underneath. While the animal grazed, Nate sat under the spreading limbs of a high pine and made his plans.

The best time to try and snatch the captives, Nate reasoned, would be about midnight. All the Bloods would be asleep by then except for the brave chosen to keep watch. Provided the escape went undetected, he'd head south immediately and take the two whites to his cabin. Fort Laramie would be the next stop. There they could arrange for an escort to the States.

Pulling his buffalo robe tighter around him, Nate leaned back against the tree trunk and closed his eyes.

A short rest was in order so he'd be fresh and alert later. But he couldn't sleep, no matter how hard he tried. The thought of tangling with the Bloods had him on edge.

After a while Nate rose and moved into the open. Vivid streaks of red, pink, and orange had transformed the western sky into a striking quilt work of marvelous colors, courtesy of the sun which hung suspended above the horizon. He went to the stallion, opened a parfleche, and took out some pemmican. Of all Indian food, this was one of Nate's favorites. It was made by pulverizing strips of buffalo jerky and mixing the powdered meat with fat and dried, ground berries. Not only was pemmican tasty, but it kept for months. Winona had insisted he take most of their meager supply when he went off hunting, but he had refused to leave them with hardly any food at all and taken just enough to tide him over in an emergency.

Nate savored every bite as he made a circuit of the clearing, stamping his feet now and then to warm his legs. The temperature was already starting to drop. Once the sun was gone, it would plummet to near zero, which would work in his favor. The Bloods would be bundled under their blankets and robes and consequently less likely to detect him.

Thoughts of little Evelyn filled Nate's mind. She was still nursing, but in time he'd have another mouth to feed, and the prospect was daunting. In the summer months, when game was plentiful, and berries, persimmons and other fruits, and edible roots and stalks were abundant, feeding his family was no problem. But in the winter, with game scarce and the plant life dormant, he was often hard pressed to keep the bellies of his loved ones full.

Nor did Nate suffer this hardship alone. All Indian tribes, whether they dwelled on the plains or up in the

mountains, knew lean times during the cold months. The
grim specter of possible starvation hung constantly over
their heads from December to March, from the Long
Night Moon to the Awaking Moon. March, in fact, was
known to all tribes as the Hunger Moon.

Presently, sparkling stars blossomed in the inky sky.
Nate checked all of his guns, insuring they were loaded.
Then, taking the stallion's reins, he led the animal westward and spent the next hour and a half working his way
in a wide loop around the Blood encampment. It took so
long because he had to skirt the hill flanking them to the
west, and once in the trees north of their position, he had
to exercise extreme caution. Leaving the stallion secured
to a limb, he continued on. The wind was blowing from
the northwest to the southeast, causing him to worry the
Blood mounts would get a whiff of his scent and act up,
but he was able to reach a thicket within 20 yards of the
tethered animals without mishap.

There Nate made himself as comfortable as he could,
his chin resting on his forearms, and bided his time until
midnight. The Bloods were all talking and joking, in
fine spirits, no doubt anticipating the warm reception
they'd receive when they returned to their village with
two white prisoners. They generally ignored Elden and
Selena, who in turn lay quietly, although Elden time and
again glanced at the surrounding forest in hopeful anticipation. Nate was glad none of the Bloods noticed, or they
might have become suspicious.

In due course the Bloods turned in. First a few, then
more and more, until a single stocky brave armed with
a bow was the sole man awake. He sat close to the
fire, a robe over his shoulders, his back to the captives. Every so often he'd feed a small branch to the
flames or glance over his shoulder to check on Selena
and Elden.

Nate rose and silently retraced his steps to where he had tied the stallion. Shrugging out of his robe, he rolled it up and secured it on the horse. His mittens went into a parfleche. Then, the Hawken in his left hand, he made for the log behind which he had hidden earlier in the day. As he slid into place behind it, he heard the man and woman whispering.

"—tell you our mysterious benefactor isn't going to show," Elden was saying bitterly. "The man must have been a coward at heart. He's abandoned us to a horrible fate."

"A coward wouldn't have taken the risk he did by coming in so close to these Indians," Selena stated.

"Then where is he? Why hasn't he freed us yet? He told us he'd be back after dark, remember?"

"Be patient."

"How can I twiddle my thumbs when my life hangs in the balance? I don't want to die!"

Nate wanted to punch Elden in the mouth to shut the whiner up before the guard heard them. Bloods weren't fools. The brave would wonder why they were jabbering and walk over to investigate. Nate had to work fast.

Letting go of the Hawken, he drew his butcher knife and crawled around the end of the log. The flickering edge of the firelight played over the man and woman, showing the fear on Elden's face and the grim resolve on Selena's. Nate was still in deep shadow, virtually invisible. Advancing slowly, he wormed his body through the deep snow. The next instant Elden saw him and uttered a loud gasp.

Over by the fire, the warrior suddenly stood and turned. Brow furrowed, he hefted his bow and strode directly toward the captives.

And Nate.

Chapter Two

Discovery was imminent. All the warrior had to do was take a few more steps and he'd detect the outline of the mountain man's body. Nate King tensed and began to twist around, intending to dart behind the log, knowing he'd probably be spotted right away. Just as he moved, though, the woman named Selena hurled her bound body to the right, away from him, and rolled over and over across the carpet of snow. Nate kept going, his eyes on the brave.

The Blood gave a grunt and ran to intercept her.

In a twinkling Nate was safely under cover. He put his eye to the corner of the log in time to see the warrior catch Selena and seize her by the front of her coat. She tried to bite his wrist and received a slap across the face for her trouble. Then, scowling fiercely, the stocky Blood dragged her back to Elden's side and roughly shoved her down. The warrior snapped a few words and motioned sharply, clearly ordering her to stay put or suffer severe consequences.

Elden was a statue, immobile with fear. He came to life only when the Blood stalked off. Licking his lips, he glanced at Selena and whispered, "Damn you and your recklessness! You could have gotten us both killed."

"Be quiet, you fool."

A few of the Bloods had stirred and sat up during the commotion. Nate was relieved to see them lying back down. All, that is, except a tall brave who conversed briefly with the guard, the two of them staring at the captives the whole time. Nate was afraid they'd move the man and woman closer to the fire. But after a minute the tall one reclined on his side and the guard took up his previous position.

Nate dared not do anything until he felt certain the warriors who had been awakened were again in deepest sleep. He knew they'd be restless for a spell, likely to snap awake at the least little noise. All thanks to Elden.

Not three minutes had gone by when that particular gentleman whispered harshly, "Mister, are you still there? What in the hell are you waiting for? Get us out of here."

Nate heard Selena speak so softly he couldn't distinguish her words, and after that there wasn't a sound out of Elden. The wind intensified, rustling and shaking the nearby trees. Nate noticed some of the stars being blotted out by low clouds, possible harbingers of an approaching storm. This brought a scowl to his face. The last thing he wanted was to be stranded in a blizzard with the two greenhorns.

The camp had long been tranquil and the guard was slumped over as if dozing when Nate crawled into the open for the second time. Holding the knife in front of him, he inched to the captives, both of whom were wide awake and observing his every movement with bated breaths. Elden was the closest, but Nate went right past him and over to Selena. Putting a finger to his lips to enjoin silence, he applied the finely honed blade to the cord binding her.

"Hurry, stranger!" Elden squeaked. "For God's sake, hurry!"

Nate's knife flicked out and the point touched the dandy's throat. "Another word out of you and I'll leave you here," he growled. "I'm not about to get myself killed on your account."

Elden gulped.

"You'll have to excuse him, sir," Selena said demurely. "He's never been this afraid before."

Lowering the knife, Nate concentrated on her bounds to the exclusion of all else, slicing carefully in order to avoid accidentally cutting her skin. In short order the cord was lying in a loose pile. He took her hand and crawled at her side to the safety of the log, then went back for Elden.

The man's eyes were as wide as walnuts. His face glistened with perspiration despite the frigid air, and his breaths rasped from his quaking chest as Nate sawed back and forth. When the cord finally parted, Elden would have scrambled for the log had Nate not grabbed his shoulder and held him in place. Nate gestured for the man to go slow, and after Elden nodded his understanding, Nate preceded him.

Now speed was essential. Nate had to get the pair out of there before the guard noticed they were gone. Reclaiming the Hawken, Nate rose until he was doubled over, then beckoned for them to follow him and entered the forest. Once screened by the snow-laden tress and bushes, he went faster, but not as fast as he would have liked. Elden and Selena slowed him down. Both had been trussed up for hours on end and their circulation was greatly impaired. They walked awkwardly at first, and would have fallen several times had he not rendered assistance.

Nate chafed at the delay. At any moment he expected to hear a shrill whoop of alarm. Amazingly, they reached the stallion in one piece and he faced the pair. "I want the two of you to stay put while I fetch you some horses."

"You have others hidden close by?" Elden asked.

"No."

"But where . . . ?" Elden said, and stopped short when insight dawned. "Lord, no! You're going to try and steal mounts from the Indians!"

"I don't have much choice. Horses don't have the knack of growing on trees yet," Nate declared as he headed off.

"It's too dangerous!" Elden protested. "If you're caught, what happens to us? We wouldn't last a day without your help."

"I'll be back."

"No!" Elden said. "Our welfare must be your first concern. I won't permit it."

Nate paused. "I'm not one for giving advice unless it's asked for, but in your case I'll make an exception. The lady told you a while ago to keep your mouth shut. I'd do that, if I was you, unless you think you can find your way out of these mountains alone." Without waiting for a response, Nate hastened through the murky woods to where he could see the row of horses. Most were like the Bloods, asleep. A few were chewing on grass and strips of sweet cottonwood bark the warriors had gathered and piled high before night fell.

Like a stalking panther Nate glided from cover to cover until he was within a couple of yards of the animals.

He saw several of them prick up their ears and sniff the air, and knew they were aware that he was there. None of them, however, nickered, or otherwise displayed any agitation that might rouse the Bloods.

Nate stepped into the open. He would have to take the two mounts at the end of the line and hope they wouldn't resist. As he neared the first one, a sorrel, the horse swung its head around and regarded him intently. "There, there," he whispered, relying on the soothing tone of his voice to alleviate any fears the animal had. "I won't hurt you. Honest." He leaned the Hawken against his leg and placed a palm on the sorrel's neck. Its skin rippled but it made no sound. Smiling, he stroked it with one hand while untying the rope rein with the other. He glanced at the camp.

Across the way, the Blood on guard unexpectedly stood and stretched. He moved a few feet, then leaned down to pick up several branches. As he did, his gaze strayed to the spot where the captives had been lying.

"Damn," Nate said.

The Blood straightened and vented a piercing shriek that brought every last warrior off the ground ready for battle. They commenced shouting back and forth and looking every which way.

Nate took a calculated gamble. Drawing his left flint-lock, he cocked the piece, held it aloft, and fired into the air while simultaneously screeching like a tormented banshee. The string of stallions, prone to be skittish under the best of circumstances, whinnied and tore at their ropes. Fully half broke loose and were galvanized into flight, fleeing back across the open space toward the startled Bloods. Nate lunged at the second horse in line, but the animal jerked backwards, tearing its rope loose, and joined the panicked flight of the others.

Firming his hold on the sorrel, Nate dashed into the trees. A look back showed the Bloods were in turmoil, either striving to stop their fleeing mounts or diving out of the way of flying hoofs. He plunged into the forest, angling for the spot where the two pilgrims were waiting. To his rear rose bedlam, the frenzied shouts of the warriors mingled with the strident whinnies of the horses.

Nate knew it was only a matter of time before the Bloods reorganized and came after him. They'd readily find his trail in the snow, so he must put as much distance behind him as swiftly as he could. He wended among the trees, hauling the sorrel in his wake, and came to where he had left the man and woman. Only they weren't there. Nor was his own stallion. He glanced at the ground, thinking perhaps he was mistaken and it wasn't the right place, but there, visible even in the gloomy woods, was the trampled, torn-up snow. Shock shot through him as he realized they had stolen his horse and fled.

The shock, though, lasted but a few seconds, and was replaced by simmering anger. Nate swung onto the sorrel and leaned down to study the tracks. The trail bore to the northwest, which was added proof the pair had no wilderness savvy whatsoever since they were heading *toward* Blood country rather than away from it. Prodding the sorrel in the flanks with his heels, Nate headed in pursuit. They couldn't be far ahead of him, he reasoned, so he should be able to overtake them quickly.

Riding on a moonless night was a hazardous proposition, as Nate well knew. Holes and ruts were difficult to discern, and obstacles such as low logs and boulders, blending as they did into the inky shadows, were harder to avoid. He rode with every sense primed, the Hawken across his thighs.

The course the pair had taken took Nate around a hill, through a gap, and along a winding valley. There the wind lashed him mercilessly, stinging his exposed cheeks with freezing blasts. Since his robe was tied to the stallion, his sole protection against the merciless elements was his buckskin shirt and pants. Ordinarily they kept him quite warm, but now, with the temperature continuing to steadily plummet, he was feeling the numbing effect of the cold, a condition that promised to worsen unless he donned more clothes or made a fire. But Nate wasn't about to stop to do the latter, not when he had two treacherous greenhorns to catch and a pack of bloodthirsty Bloods soon to be after his scalp.

All of a sudden there was a commotion ahead of him. Nate reined up and raised the Hawken as a large form crashed through underbrush to his left. He had his thumb on the icy hammer and was cocking it when the form emerged and he recognized the outline of a horse. Not just any horse either. It was his stallion.

Nate saw the stallion start to swing around him. Apparently it hadn't caught his scent and didn't know if he was friendly or not. So, counting on the sound of his voice to reassure it, he said, "Where do you think you're going in such an all-fired hurry?"

The stallion promptly stopped, bobbed its head a few times, and advanced warily until Nate touched its muzzle. "Yes, it's me," he said. "Don't you know better than to go traipsing off with strangers?"

Nate petted his horse a few times, then transferred from the sorrel to the stallion by simply sliding from one to the other. His robe had not been touched, and he lost no time in slipping it on. Then, clutching the sorrel's reins, he turned and entered the underbrush, backtracking the stallion.

Not a minute later Nate heard voices. Slowing, he pinpointed the location, and rode toward a hill on his left. Partway up the slope indistinct figures materialized, shuffling through the deep snow toward him. He stayed where he was, concealed by the night, and heard an angry exchange.

"—never should have ridden off. the way we did," Selena was chiding her companion.

"You heard the shot and all that wild yelling," Elden replied. "Whoever that man was, he's dead. We had to save ourselves or we would have suffered the same fate."

"We still may, now that the horse has run off," Selena said. "I told you this slope was too steep and slippery, but you wouldn't listen. As usual."

"That's not true. You always get your way."

"If that was the case," Selena snapped, "we wouldn't be in this fix, would we?" She paused. "Sometimes I wonder why I tolerate your childish behavior the way I do. You haven't done a thing right since you learned to walk."

"Don't start with your criticisms again," Elden retorted. "I've had about enough . . ." He broke off and halted in midstride. "Look! There's someone below us!"

Nate sat stock still and said nothing. He swore he could see Elden quaking in abject fear, which pleased him immensely. From their discussion, he gathered that it had been Elden's idea to ride off and leave him; putting a scare into the coward was fitting justice.

Presently Selena broke the silence. "It's him, you fool! The man who helped us." Hiking the hem of her dress, she ran to the base of the hill. "Thank God you're all right! I was so worried!"

"Then why didn't you wait for me?" Nate responded.

"I'm sorry. I should have," Selena admitted, "but I couldn't let Elden ride off by himself. He's helpless without me around to look after him."

Motioning at the sorrel, Nate said, "Climb up. We'll talk more about this later. First we have to lose the Bloods."

"What about me?" Elden had found his voice. He hurriedly waddled over, puffing like a steam engine.

"What about you?" Nate rejoined.

"You surely don't expect me to walk!"

"I don't expect anything from you, mister. You're all on your own as far as I'm concerned," Nate informed him.

"On my own?" Elden surveyed the ominous veil of darkness enveloping them. "You can't be serious! You wouldn't desert me in the middle of nowhere with a bunch of demented heathens no doubt hunting us down at this very minute?"

"Watch me," Nate said. Shifting in the saddle, he saw Selena trying to mount the war horse but having a problem because the animal was shying away at each attempt. "Try the other side," he suggested.

"I beg your pardon?"

"That animal won't let you get up unless you do it from the Indian side," Nate explained, and when she looked at him as if confused, he elaborated. "Indians always mount from the right side, not the left like we do. Try it."

Selena had the reins in one hand. Moving around the sorrel, she got a grip on its mane, threw back her leg, and swung gracefully astride the now docile horse. "Thank you," she said. "All the times I've watched them and I forgot!"

Nate turned his stallion and suppressed a grin when Elden let out a frightened yelp.

"Wait! You can't do this! I'm a white man too! You can't just leave me here to die!"

"You left *me*," Nate reminded him.

"I thought you were dead!" Elden wailed. "And I didn't want those savages getting their hands on Selena. You would have done the same thing if you'd been in my shoes."

Nate swung toward the pilgrim so abruptly that Elden took a half step backward. "No, I wouldn't, mister. One of the first lessons a man learns out here is to stand on his own two feet, to meet hardship head-on. Not to turn tail just because his hide is in danger."

"I'm sorry. Can't you find it in your heart to forgive me?"

Before Nate could answer, Selena interjected a comment, saying, "I can't just ride off and leave him. And I don't really think you intend doing so either."

"I won't run out on you again," Elden said hastily. "I promise. I'll do whatever you want." He clasped his hands and implored, "Please. Please. I'll beg if I have to. But don't forsake me!"

Seldom had such coarse contempt filled Nate as at that very moment. He could barely conceal his disdain as he gestured at the sorrel and declared, "I need to be able to move quickly if those Bloods catch us, so the two of you will have to ride double. Climb up with the lady."

"She's no lady," Elden said, mustering a grin. "She's my sister."

"Honestly," Selena said. "Sometimes you can be as crude as tavern trash."

Nate moved off, bearing to the southeast, picturing in his mind's eye the route he desired to take. He ignored the greenhorns, even when they drew alongside him, although he did note that Elden was now in the saddle,

Selena clinging to him from behind. The man rode slop-
pily, his legs jouncing uncontrollably, his arms pumping
as if he was trying to draw water from a well. It was a
wonder the sorrel didn't attempt to buck him off!

"What's that?" Selena suddenly asked.

The same sounds had reached Nate's ears. A lot of
horses were racing in their general direction from the
south. He cut to the left, nearly colliding with the sorrel, and moved at a trot into thick pines. Here the going
was slower, but they were invisible to hostile eyes in the
valley. He changed direction again, turning to the right,
staying within a dozen yards of the tree line in case they
had to make for open ground in a hurry.

"Can I ask you a question?" Elden whispered.

"Just one."

"I'm afraid we haven't been properly introduced.
What's your name? I'm Elden Leonard, and this is
Selena."

"Nate King."

"We can't ever express how truly grateful we are for
all you've done," Elden said cheerfully. "Those devils
had us in their clutches for ages, and you can't imagine
the ordeal we've been through. Why, one—"

"Quit your chawing and keep your eyes peeled," Nate
interrupted brusquely. "We're far from safe yet."

"My chawing?"

"Close your mouth. I'll let you know when you can
talk."

"If you don't mind my saying so, Mr. King, you have
a very gruff manner at times. A little common courtesy,
sir, would go a long way to—"

"Elden?"

"Yes?"

"Shut the hell up," Nate commanded. He was trying to
mark the progress of the Bloods and couldn't with all the

jabbering. Just his luck, he reflected, to fall in with a fool who loved to hear himself chatter. Nate came to a narrow gap between the trees and halted. Off to the southwest a moving pinpoint of light flared, followed seconds later by several more, clustered together and swaying as if in the wind.

"What in the world are those?" Elden blurted out.

"Torches," Nate answered. "The Bloods are using them to track us." Frowning, he rode to the very edge of the pines. From this vantage point he could see the group of warriors several hundred yards away, rushing up the valley. The Bloods wouldn't reach the hill where the tracks changed direction for another two minutes yet. "Stay close to me," he cautioned, and forsook the cover of the forest for the open grass. Then, facing to the south, he brought the stallion to a gallop.

Nate had been unable to count the number of warriors in the party, but he was sure some were missing, perhaps still chasing their frightened animals or else waiting back at the camp. There might be stragglers also, braves who had caught their horses too late to join the main party and who were hastening to catch up. He must stay vigilant.

They were almost to the mouth of the valley when Nate heard a shout. Looking around, he saw a solitary Blood speeding to head them off. He brought the Hawken up, cocking it as he did, took a bead on the warrior's torso, and when the now-screeching brave was only 15 yards off, stroked the trigger. At the sharp retort the Blood pitched rearward in a whirl of arms and legs.

"Ride!" Nate said, suiting his actions to his words. He flew across the snow-covered ground. The Leonards imitated his example, doing well despite their inexperience.

To the northwest rose feral yips and enraged howls as the Bloods realized their quarry had outfoxed them. The dancing balls of light reversed course.

"They're after us!" Elden cried.

Nate was busy seeking the gap. Shrouded in black as it was, the task was next to impossible. He had to rely on the instinctive sense of direction he had developed during his years in the wilderness and hope he reached it before the Bloods reached them.

"Oh, God! We're doomed!" Elden shouted.

"Quiet, damn you!" Nate said over his shoulder. Out of the corner of his eye he spied what appeared to be a break in the trees, and thinking he'd found the gap, he guided the stallion into it. Too late he saw his eyes had tricked him, that the break was actually a small half-moon clearing that bordered a high hill. Hauling on the reins, he brought the stallion to a sliding halt and turned.

The Bloods were less than a hundred yards distant. Outracing them was out of the question.

Nate glanced right and left. There was nowhere to take cover, nowhere to make a fight of it.

"What do we do?" Elden yelled. "What do we do?"

About to gallop along the base of the hill, Nate spotted more braves directly in front of him, stragglers barring his path. He went to snap off a shot, then remembered both his Hawken and one of his pistols were spent. Only one flintlock was still loaded. At that instant, arcing out of the sky, a whizzing arrow appeared as a pale, streaking blur not more than eight feet away, coming straight at his head.

Chapter Three

Almost a decade of wilderness living had honed Nate King's body to a razor's edge. His muscles had been hardened by constant hard toil, his sinews sharpened to where his physical coordination was superb. In order to survive, he had developed his strength, stamina, and speed to a degree few other whites could equal. Necessity had forged him on the anvil of survival, and it could not have been otherwise, for those men who didn't adapt to the harsh mistress called Nature were inevitably crushed by her.

So exceptionally keen were Nate's reflexes that his body was bending a fraction of a second after his eyes registered the threat to his life. A heartbeat later the deadly shaft struck the top of his beaver hat, transfixing it from front to back and propelling it from his head.

With Indians converging from two directions and trees blocking retreat on the third side, Nate had no choice but

31

to bring the stallion around and gallop toward the slope behind them. Elden was right on his heels, stark terror temporarily making a master horseman out of him.

The Bloods were yipping like a pack of ravenous wolves. More arrows rained down, but wide of their mark.

Nate took the slope on the fly and goaded the stallion upward. Mighty hoofs driving, it struggled to keep its footing. Snow sprayed rearward. Nate glanced back and saw the sorrel losing ground. Burdened as it was with two riders, the Indian mount slipped and floundered. Nate's eyes flicked to the stragglers, who were closer than the main body, and in desperation, hoping to forestall capture or worse, he whipped out the loaded pistol and took hasty aim.

At the blast of smoke and lead, the foremost warrior fell. Immediately the remaining stragglers scattered into the nearest trees, and the main group slowed.

Nate had bought precious seconds at best, and now all three of his guns were virtually useless. He had to reload. But he dared not stop. Legs slapping the stallion's side, he urged the big black horse toward the crest. A frantic neigh below, however, drew him up shy of his goal.

The sorrel had gone down. Both Elden and Selena had been thrown clear and were rising, their clothes caked with snow. Legs thrashing, the sorrel was striving to regain its footing but unable to get a purchase.

"Help it!" Nate bellowed, jumping to the ground. He ran back to the frantic animal, seized the bridle, and heaved. Elden was standing a few feet off, gaping in dumb horror. "Help me, you idiot!" Nate roared.

Elden only moved when Selena gave him a rough shove. Stumbling forward, he grabbed the other side of the bridle and strained upward, his face going crimson from the exertion.

More by its own efforts than theirs, the sorrel managed to surge to its feet. Nate shoved the reins at Elden and snapped, "Lead it to the top." Then, whirling, he faced the charging Bloods as an arrow thudded into the frozen earth within inches of his moccasins.

Some of the stragglers had dismounted, the better to use their bows. The main group was fanning out, taking their sweet time about it because they believed the three whites were cornered. One brave, more rash than the rest, was well in advance of his fellows and waving a lance overhead as he bore down on the hill.

Nate did the only thing he could. He flung the Hawken to his shoulder in a blatant bluff, and the brave, seeing the motion, promptly swerved into the trees on the left. Grinning grimly, Nate moved backward, keeping his empty rifle trained on the warriors. Since they didn't know his guns were empty, they were being prudently cautious.

And there was another factor involved. In most tribes, the men were greatly outnumbered by the women. Ceaseless warfare, raids on enemy villages, hunting buffalo, and other hazardous activities all took a terrible toll on the male population. Consequently, Indians regarded the loss of even a single brave as bad medicine, to be avoided at all costs. When engaged in warfare, they seldom took senseless, reckless risks, although at times their innate courage inspired them to commit audacious acts.

So, for the moment, Nate held the Bloods at bay. A dozen more arrows thudded into the ground as he retreated, the barbed rain not ceasing until he was close to the crest.

Selena held the reins of the stallion. Her brother was leaning against the sorrel, seemingly on the verge of collapse. "What do we do now?" he whined.

Instead of responding, Nate shed his robe and began reloading the Hawken, his fingers moving with practiced precision. Since there was so little light, he had to guess at the proper amount of black powder.

"Didn't you hear me?" Elden said after a minute.

"We wait and see what they do," Nate answered without looking up from his ammo pouch.

"That's all?"

"What would you suggest?"

"I don't know. But waiting to be slaughtered isn't very wise, in my estimation."

Nate began extracting the ramrod from its housing under the rifle barrel. "We can ride on back down there and have them shoot us so full of arrows we'll look like oversized porcupines, or we can sit tight and use our noggins."

Elden chewed on his lower lip, the whites of his eyes showing. "Why don't we go down the other side of this hill? We might be able to get away."

"With the two of you riding double?" Nate shook his head. "They'd be on us before we went a quarter of a mile."

"I just don't think—" Elden started to say, but his sister cut him off.

"No, you don't. So do us all a favor and let Mr. King figure out what we should do without being pestered by your prattle. He's our only hope of getting out of this fix alive."

There was a swirl of activity at the base of the slope. The Bloods were spreading out around the hill, their intent as transparent as ice on a lake; they were going to completely ring the hill to prevent escape.

Selena, always the more astute of the pair, divined the Indians' purpose first and inquired, "Will they come up after us once they close the trap?"

"Depends on how patient they feel," Nate said, busy with a pistol. "They might try to wait us out, just sit down there until thirst and hunger drive us down into their arms. Or they might rush us come daylight." He shrugged. "They might even try to drop us with arrows once they can see clear enough to shoot straight."

"Oh, mercy," Elden breathed. "To be struck down in the prime of my manhood! Who would have thought it?"

"We're not dead yet," Nate said.

"Your optimism, sir, flies in the face of logic."

Selena smiled at Nate. "My brother can be unbearable at times, I know, but he means well. He's really a gentle soul who wouldn't hurt anyone."

"Then he has no business being in these mountains," Nate remarked. "The Rockies are no place for dreamers and simpletons.

Elden's spine stiffened. "I resent that," he said.

"Get your dander up all you want. But you can't change the fact that out here only the strong survive. Weaklings are just naturally weeded out."

"*Spare me* your frontier philosophy," Elden said indignantly. "It's all a matter of what you're accustomed to. I dare say I'd be more at home in New York City than you could ever hope to be."

"I was born and raised there."

"You were?" Elden said incredulously. He studied Nate from head to toe. "What brought you to this sorry state?"

"Elden!" Selena declared.

"I don't mean to be insulting," her brother said. "I'm merely puzzled as to why any sane man would forsake such a city for this godforsaken wilderness."

Nate shifted. "If we make it out of this with our hair intact, I'll tell you." He walked to the highest point of the crest, working on the pistol as he did. Shadowy figures flitted about at the bottom. The Bloods were taking their positions. He watched them for a while, weighing the alternatives open to him, seeking a way to save himself and the two Easterners.

"How can you act so calm at such a time?" Elden wanted to know. "Doesn't the idea of dying disturb you in the least?"

"If a man spends all his time fretting about dying, he doesn't get much living done," Nate answered.

"Lord. You are a regular fount of wisdom."

Only an arrogant city-bred popinjay, Nate reflected, would antagonize his savior. He moved further off so he could think undisturbed. The Bloods now ringed the entire hill, the braves spaced at 30- or 40-yard intervals. They didn't give any evidence of being eager to mount an all-out rush—yet. He made a circuit of the crown and returned to the anxious pair Fate had thrust upon him. "We can breathe easy for a spell," he announced. "Doesn't look as if they'll attack before first light."

Elden snorted. "If I believed in God, I suppose now would be the time to make my peace with my Maker."

Nate walked away and gazed heavenward. Clouds dominated the sky, and the wind was growing ever stronger. His hunch about a storm might prove correct. If so, it could prove to be the source of their salvation, depending on the timing. Would the snow commence falling before dawn or afterward? Soft footfalls intruded on his musing.

"No matter what happens, I wanted you to know I appreciate all you've done for us," Selena Leonard said softly. "Especially in tolerating my brother. He can be a terrible burden." She sighed. "I should know. I've been looking after him since we were children, and there isn't a day that doesn't go by where I don't feel like pulling my hair out in frustration."

"Why put up with him?" Nate idly asked.

"We're family, and family should always stick together no matter what comes along. Our parents taught us that and we live by it."

Nate thought of his own brothers, with whom he had once been close, all grown aloof since the death of their folks. Admiration for Selena's steadfast loyalty sparked him to comment, "I'd never have done what you've done. If Elden was my kin, I'd have left him years ago."

"We all have to make sacrifices sometimes," Selena said. "And believe it or not, there are times when he is a perfect dear."

Nate was going to inquire about the circumstances surrounding their capture when a snowflake hit his cheek. Tilting back his head, he was elated to see a light snowfall had begun. He rapidly finished with the last pistol, wedged it under his belt, and pivoted so he faced both greenhorns. "We're going to make a run for it if the snow gets heavier," he informed them.

"You're crazy," Elden said.

"It will be our only chance," Nate responded. "The Bloods can't hit what they can't see."

"But what if our horse slips? My sister and I would be at their mercy. No, sir. We're staying right here."

"Fine," Nate said. "Just try not to scream too loud when they overrun you come morning." Disgusted with the pudgy pilgrim's constant bickering, he walked to his stallion and checked his saddle.

Selena and her brother went off to one side. For several minutes they whispered angrily back and forth until finally Selena, her chin jutting, her eyes flashing, jabbed a finger into her brother's chest and said loud enough for

Nate to hear, "You'll do as I say, and I don't want any more guff out of you."

Nate was beginning to consider their behavior a bit peculiar. Brothers and sisters were prone to fighting a lot, as he knew from his own experience, but normally they outgrew that when they became adults. These two were always at each other's throats, and it frankly amazed him they had stayed together as long as Selena claimed. Deciding their personal affairs were rightfully none of his business, he scoured the slope on the east side, searching for obstacles they must avoid when they made their dash for freedom.

Selena came over. "My brother has agreed to do as you wish."

"Are his legs broken?" Nate asked.

"What?" Selena said, then, "Oh!" Musical laughter fluttered from her red lips. "No, but there are occasions when I'm tempted. You can't imagine how trying it is, always having to set him straight."

"I have a fair notion," Nate said dryly.

The snow was becoming heavier. Selena held a palm out to let some flakes land on her hand. "Do you honestly think we have a prayer?"

Nate stared at the Bloods, who had dismounted and tied their horses to convenient trees or brush, mulling her question. Once the warriors recovered from their initial surprise, they'd go for their mounts on the run. At the most, he could count on a 30-second head start, which wasn't much at all when dealing with seasoned braves, most of whom learned to ride expertly before their tenth birthday.

"Do you?" Selena repeated.

"A slim one," Nate conceded. "Just remember. Whatever happens, don't let your brother stop. Keep going until I tell you otherwise."

"What if something happens to you?"

"Then you can rest when you reach the Mississippi," Nate joked, since the river lay hundreds of miles to the east. A gust of wind fanned his hair, reminding him of his lost hat, and he brushed his bangs from his eyes with his left hand. Visibility was gradually diminishing as the snow worsened.

A low nicker brought Nate around in time to catch Elden Leonard in the act of climbing on the sorrel. "No!" he said curtly. "Not until I give the word."

"What difference does it make?"

"If the Bloods should see you, they might guess what we're up to."

"But my backside is cold and the horse is so warm."

"I'm not in the mood to argue," Nate warned, and glanced at Selena. "So he's going to do as I wish from here on out? Is that what you told me?"

"I tried."

Moments later a tremendous gust of northerly air whipped the snow on the ground and the flakes in the air into an agitated frenzy. Nate squinted down at the bottom of the hill, which was now totally obscured by the building storm. He'd wait a bit, he decided, to be safe. Suddenly a warm hand slipped into his, startling him.

"I'm scared," Selena said in a low tone, so low her brother couldn't hear.

"We'll be all right," Nate assured her. He felt decidedly uncomfortable having her touch him, but out of common courtesy he made no attempt to pull away. She must, he imagined, be thoroughly frightened by her ordeal, and since her brother wasn't offering her any comfort, he might as well be polite.

"If we do get out alive, I hope I can find some way to repay your kindness."

"There's no need," Nate said as inspiration struck. "Just having a female visitor to keep my wife company for a few days will be thanks enough. It isn't often we get folks stopping by our little cabin."

"You're married?"

"To the loveliest woman on God's green earth," Nate replied. He half expected Selena to remove her hand from his, but to his amazement she actually gave him a squeeze.

"I should have known a strapping, handsome man like you would have a wife. I'm very happy for her." Selena's features were blurred by the swirling snow. "I've never found the right man for me. Frankly, I don't know if I ever will."

"Never give up hope," Nate said.

A bulky figure suddenly emerged out of the thickening white veil and grumbled, "How much longer are we going to stand here? I'm about frozen stiff, I tell you. At least we should start a fire."

"We don't have any wood," Nate mentioned. "And the wind is too strong up here." He eased his hand loose and took a few steps forward, scouring the benighted slope. Not even an eagle would be able to see more than five or six feet in the snow inundating the Rockies. So, although he still preferred to wait a while longer, Elden's tireless complaining prompted him to declare, "Mount up. We're leaving."

Elden gave a whoop of joy and took his sister's elbow to guide her to the sorrel.

Nate stepped into the stirrups, then waited for them to come alongside him. "Listen closely," he advised. "We're going to walk to the bottom and head for the trees."

"Walk?" Elden said. "Is that wise? The savages will be able to pick us off easily." He shook his head. "I say we ride just as fast as we can and don't stop until we're well in the clear."

"You were the one who was so worried about his horse falling a while ago," Nate reminded the green-horn. "Try going down this hill at a gallop and that's exactly what will happen. The Bloods will hear and be on you before you can hope to get away." He jabbed an arm at the layer of snow already covering the ground. "No, we go slow so we don't make any noise. Since this storm will hide us from them, they won't have any idea we've gone until it clears up."

"But what if we run into one of them at the bottom?" Elden's asked apprehensively.

"I know how far apart they're spaced. We should be able to go between two of them without being spotted."

"You hope."

Nate sighed. "Stay right behind me. If we become separated, I may never find you again. The storm will wipe out all your tracks."

Selena spoke. "We won't lose you. I'll see to that."

Holding the Hawken across his left leg, Nate lifted the reins and started the stallion downward at a slow walk. The swishing of the snow and the whistling of the wind were the only sounds. He peered intently ahead for any hint of movement. There was a possibility the Bloods were using the cover of the storm to their own advantage by sneaking toward the crest, and he didn't care to bump into them halfway down.

Nate had to lean back to adjust his balance as the slope steepened. His hands, no longer shielded by his fur mittens, were terribly cold, his fingertips practically frozen. His eyes played tricks on him, often mistaking elusive shadows for solid figures. He strained his ears to their limits, but heard nothing to indicate the Bloods had moved from their previous positions. Every so often he glanced around to insure the Leonards were where they should be.

Eternity became compressed into mere minutes. Nate broke out in a nervous sweat under his buckskins despite the temperature. He had to guess at how far they had gone at any given point, and by his estimation they were two thirds of the way to the bottom when another seemingly solid form appeared off to his right. Nate looked, and the skin at the back of his neck tingled.

It was a Blood, working his way uphill.

Nate braced for a shout but none came. The brave had his gaze fixed straight ahead and didn't spot them; within seconds the warrior was swallowed by the storm. Expelling the breath he hadn't realized he was holding, Nate continued lower. Just ten more yards or so, he reckoned, and they would be off the hill.

The wind, which had been howling like a lonely wolf for minutes, abruptly slackened. The falling snow still hissed, and Nate could also hear the dull clomp of hoofs. He glanced up, wishing the wind would resume.

When the change came, Nate was taken by surprise. One moment the stallion was plodding along with its body inclined, the next, Nate felt the horse level out under him, but he went a few feet before he awakened to the fact they were on flat ground again. Smiling, he twisted to check on his charges, who were right where they should be. He glimpsed Elden's frightened face, and saw Selena staring to the left. She swung her head to look at him, and as she did her eyes widened, her lips parted.

"Look out!"

Nate spun. A stocky Blood was rushing toward him, a war club upraised. Nate tried to bring the Hawken to bear, but the Blood vented a bloodcurdling shriek and launched into the air, hurtling into him like a human battering ram. Nate felt the brave's brawny arms encircle him, and then he was falling off the opposite side of the stallion.

In desperation, Nate twisted, trying to flip so the Blood would be on the bottom when they hit. In this he was only partially successful. They both smacked down on their sides. The Blood instantly pushed back and swung the war club. Nate countered by bringing up the Hawken and deflecting the blow with the rifle barrel.

Somewhere, someone was shouting.

Nate drove the rifle stock at the Blood's face, but the man jerked backward, out of reach. Scrambling to his knees, Nate blocked a second swing of the club. Then, reversing his grip, he thrust the barrel into the brave's stomach, doubling the Blood over. There was a resounding crack as the stock connected with the side of the warrior's head and the man crumpled, still game, though, as he proved by trying to slam the stout club against Nate's legs. Nate raised the Hawken aloft, then brought the stock down one last time.

The Blood went prone, blood oozing from the wound.

Pivoting, Nate saw the stallion standing a few yards off. He also saw another warrior racing toward him.

Selena and Elden Leonard, however, were gone.

Chapter Four

Nate King darted to his stallion, and was reaching for the saddle when he realized he would never make it. The second Blood was too close and notching an arrow to a sinew bowstring. Facing the brave, Nate drew his right flintlock. He cocked the hammer as the Blood raised the bow. He extended his arm as the Blood sighted along the shaft. And he squeezed the trigger a heartbeat before the Blood let fly.

The arrow flashed across the intervening space almost too swiftly for the human eye to follow. Nate tried to throw himself against the stallion so the shaft would miss, but his right foot slipped in the snow. Aghast, he saw the barbed point rip into his right shoulder and felt the jolt of impact. The flintlock was nearly torn from his grasp. He had to will himself to ignore the wound and focus on the Blood. If he didn't, another shaft would rip into his body at any moment.

Concern proved unwarranted since the lead ball had bored into the warrior's right eye and burst out the back of his cranium. He lay askew in the snow, a crimson pool framing his head.

Jamming the pistol under his belt, Nate climbed onto the stallion and headed into the storm. Much to his disbelief, there was no pain in his shoulder. Nor did he feel any blood trickling over his chest and upper arm. He counted himself fortunate the shaft had missed a vital vein or artery, and he could only pray the wound wouldn't become infected.

Nate scoured the terrain for the Leonards. Either the sorrel had been spooked by the attacking Blood and fled on its own, which Nate doubted since it was a Blood war horse, or Elden had once again displayed his yellow streak. They could have gone any which way. Nate looked and looked but there were no tracks. The snow was so heavy, it filled in prints as quickly as they were made. And the wind had increased again, lashing the loose flakes on the surface into a fine mist.

From the hill came yells in the Blood tongue. The warriors knew their prey was gone and they would soon institute a search.

Trees reared in front of Nate. He wound into them and stopped when he reached a quiet spot sheltered from the blowing snow by two wide spruce. There he slid his left hand under his robe, gingerly moving his fingers across his chest to the arrow. So numb were his fingertips by this time that he didn't perceive what had happened at first. Then the truth dawned, and Nate laughed.

The shaft had gone completely through the heavy robe, but had missed his arm by a hair. There was a slight tear in the sleeve of his buckskin shirt, nothing more.

Overjoyed, Nate grasped the shaft, and with a sharp snap, he broke off the fletching. Next, by reaching around behind him, he was able to grab the shaft above the point and work the rest of the arrow loose. He discarded both pieces and rode on.

Howling gusts tore through the trees, rattling the bony branches and the skeletal undergrowth. Nate slanted to the right, zigzagging as he sought some sign of the Leonards. The old saw about looking for a needle in a haystack came to his mind, yet he refused to quit. Without him, Elden and Selena would be dead in days. Not that Nate cared much one way or the other about Elden's welfare. Selena, though, he liked, and he sympathized with her plight. He'd save her if he could.

An hour later Nate was being nagged by growing despair. He was a mile or so from the hill and had covered twice that distance in his meandering hunt, but the Leonards had eluded him. For all he knew, the Bloods had captured them again. He toyed with the idea of going back, knowing if he did that he could wind up a captive himself.

The storm took the decision out of Nate's hands. It unexpectedly abated, the snow tapering to flakes, the wind dying to soft moans. He drew rein and rose in the stirrups to survey the countryside. An eerie stillness had seized the land, giving him the impression he was the sole living thing within miles. Then he heard a nicker to the southwest.

Friend or foe? Nate wondered as he headed in that direction. Sooner than he anticipated he spied a lone horse standing beside a pine tree. Slowly moving forward, he recognized the sorrel and saw that its reins were tangled in a tree limb. Elden and Selena were nowhere around.

The sorrel didn't resist as Nate freed the reins and led it northward, back the way he figured it had come. There were a few tracks at first, then none at all. He covered a hundred yards, and was beginning to think he had made a mistake when a squeal of delight snapped his head up.

Running toward him were Selena and Elden, both coated with white from head to toe. She had an arm around her brother's waist, supporting him, while his face was contorted in torment.

Nate galloped to them and vaulted down. "What happened?" he demanded.

"Elden rode into a low branch," Selena explained. "It knocked both of us off."

"I hurt!" her brother complained. "Oh, how I hurt! Some of my ribs must be shattered. You've got to do something to ease the pain!"

Nate gazed past them. "There's nothing we can do until we put some distance behind us. The Bloods might have heard that cry."

"Sorry," Selena said contritely. "I couldn't help myself. I was so happy to see you!"

The gleam in the woman's eyes bothered Nate, but he held his peace. In short order he had them both on the sorrel and was riding southward, sticking to the open ground where they could go faster. The snow had nearly stopped. Clouds hid the stars and constellations, so Nate had to guess at the time, which he calculated to be past three in the morning, maybe closer to four. Dawn was not far off.

A craggy mountain towered above them when Nate eventually slowed. Enormous boulders dotted a bare tract encompassing several acres. He rode into the midst of this boulder field, then wearily halted. With the aid of Selena, he lowered Elden to a strip of bare earth at the foot of an egg-shaped monolith.

"I can't bear it," the man whimpered. "Never, ever, have I been in so much pain. What shall I do?"

"Let me take a gander," Nate offered, kneeling. He lifted the coat and unbuttoned the suit. The white shirt underneath was spotless, nor were there any blood stains on the wool undershirt. "It didn't break the skin," he commented.

Consistently bitter, Elden responded, "What does a measly cut matter when a person's ribs have been caved in?"

Nate placed a hand on the left side of Elden's chest and applied pressure. "Does this make the pain worse?" When Elden shook his head, he tried another spot, and repeated the procedure until he was assured there were, in fact, no broken bones at all. He informed them of this.

"But my chest hurts, I tell you!" Elden insisted.

"No doubt it does," Nate said, rising. "Lie still and rest and you'll be fit to ride by daybreak."

"That soon?" said Selena.

"The Bloods lost three men, maybe four if that one with the split skull has died. They're craving our hair right about now, because the last thing they want is to go back to their village in shame."

"I don't understand."

"If the Bloods can count coup on us, if they can take my scalp and Elden's and take you captive, it will make up in part for the loss of several braves. Instead of going back to their tribe in disgrace, their people will sing their praises as mighty warriors. So they won't quit searching for us for a long time. We have to make tracks."

"How long will it take us to reach your cabin?"

"Two days at the most."

Elden, grunting, propped himself up on an elbow. "Do you have a washtub? A hot bath would rejuvenate me completely."

"There's a lake you can bathe in if you want."

"You must be jesting. No one could swim outdoors in this weather without freezing to death."

"I do it all the time. So do the Indians. It hardens you against the cold."

"Rubbish. And even if that were true, I'm not about to bathe in water that reeks from fish! I'd come out smelling worse than when I went in."

"Then stay dirty. It's your body and you can do what you want," Nate said. "But when you get whiffy, keep downwind from the horses. They'll spook sometimes if they smell a skunk or other polecat."

"Hmmmmmph!" was all Elden said.

Nate took the Hawken and moved off a dozen yards to make a circuit of their hideaway. He listened long and hard but heard no faint hoofbeats. Satisfied the Bloods hadn't found their trail yet, he retraced his steps and found Elden Leonard sound asleep. Selena was leaning against the boulder, her eyes hooded in shadow. "You should try to get some rest yourself," he suggested. "We're going to be in the saddle almost all day."

"I tried and I couldn't. Besides, I wanted to ask you a few questions."

"What about?"

"You. Your past specifically. I'm as curious as my brother. What brought you out here? And why do you stay when you could live back in the States in civilized society?"

Cradling the rifle in his arms, Nate hesitated before answering. He wanted to inform her that in the wilderness folks didn't go around prying into the private matters of others, that in fact doing so was downright unhealthy at times, but he didn't. She was new to the mountains, and as such ignorant of the unwritten etiquette practiced by whites and Indians alike. He excused her prying because she was a greenhorn, and a woman, and he answered simply, "I like it here."

"You like wearing animal skins for clothes? You like having to hunt for your food all the time? And you like having to always be on your guard against hostile heathens?"

"I like being free."

Selena stepped closer, her expression one of burning intensity. "Wouldn't you be just as free in the States as you are here? Wasn't that why America fought the Revolution?"

"Americans fought the Revolution because they were tired of being governed by the ruling class of another country. When they won, a new ruling class sprang up right here, and this class has run things ever since."

"What a peculiar idea," Selena said. "You are most mystifying, Nate King. At times you act and talk like a typical frontier ruffian, and at other times you have the air of an educated man. Which are you?"

"A little of both," Nate admitted. "As for your question about freedom, the answer is no, I wouldn't be as free in the States as I am here. Back there we have politicians making more and more laws each and every day, telling people how they should live whether the people want to live that way or not." He paused and gestured at the lofty mountain. "Out here there are no laws. Every man and woman lives by their own personal code. There's no one looking over their shoulders to make sure they live a certain way. They can do as they please provided they don't go over the line that can get them killed."

"Fascinating," Selena said.

"I'm just thankful I discovered the wilderness when I did," Nate went on in a rush of enthusiasm for the subject. "Back in New York City I was a slave to others and didn't even realize it. Everyone from my father to my fiancée wanted me to be the way they wanted me to be, and they gave no thought at all to my own feelings. I had to dress a certain way, act a certain way. I was a puppet, nothing more."

"Aren't you exaggerating just a bit? We all have certain responsibilities, certain—"

Nate was so engrossed in their conversation he almost missed the distant crack of a hoof striking a rock. He held up his hand for silence and swiveled his head to one side. There was only silence now, but he knew what he had heard. "Wake your brother," he stated. "We have to get out of here."

"I'm already awake, King," Elden declared gruffly. "I only dozed off for a minute." He yawned. "What's wrong now? Why the rush?"

"The Bloods," Nate said, climbing onto the stallion.

For once Elden offered no objections. He was mounted, his sister too, and ready to depart in a matter of seconds.

The south side of the boulder field flanked a forested ridge linked to the mountain. Nate followed a game trail to the top, a trail he would not have found had not several deer used it within the past hour and left clear prints. From the vantage point of the rim, he scoured the area to the north and caught sight of two Bloods winding cautiously among the boulders. Only two, though, leading him to surmise the pair had been sent on ahead to track the greenhorns and him down. The rest, he figured, must be tending to the brave he had smashed with the rifle. They'd catch up soon enough.

From the ridge, Nate rode to the southeast, into a narrow valley which in turn brought them to an extraordinarily rough mountainous stretch just as the new day dawned. Jagged pinnacles blanketed in white thrust into the dispersing clouds. Spacious slopes carpeted with snow were preternaturally still. The range was devoid of life, as quiet as the grave.

Nate frequently scanned the heights, remembering the time he had been caught in an avalanche. The memory gave him an idea, and within the hour he came on a defile that promised to be the answer to their prayers. Above it, on either side, perched massive banks of precariously balanced snow.

"We're going through there?" Elden broke his long silence. "What is it about you? Do you *want* to die?"

Dark shadows enclosed Nate within their dank folds as he slowly advanced. The air was positively frigid, since there the sun seldom penetrated. It was like voyaging into the depths of a damp cave. He had to crane his head back to see the top, and he was unable to suppress a slight shudder at the mental image of what would occur should the snow cascade down before he was through to the other side.

The bottom of the defile was practically devoid of snow. Isolated rocks and boulders littered the way, debris that had plunged from on high long ago.

Nate went 20 yards, then looked back. He was angered to see Elden had not yet entered and he gestured for them to follow him. Elden shook his head, eliciting a slap on the shoulder from Selena, who then pointed into the opening and said something. Elden shook his head again. Nate was all set to turn around and drag the flabby Easterner in by his hair, if need be, when Selena flailed her legs, goading the sorrel into a walk. Elden froze.

The farther Nate went, the colder it became. His breath formed into fluffy puffs that seemed to hang suspended before him. He saw tiny icicles clinging to both walls, and partway along he spied a small pool of frozen water, which he skirted.

Suddenly there was a muted rumbling from overhead. Nate glanced aloft in alarm, dreading an avalanche, but the snow remained where it was. He was strongly tempted to break into a gallop, yet checked the impulse, fully aware the pounding of hoofs might be all that was needed to precipitate disaster.

When, at long, long last, Nate emerged into the sunlight, he exhaled in relief and reined up to wait for the Leonards. They were moving at a snail's pace, Elden timidly gaping at the snowcapped heights. Selena was trying to hurry them along, but every time she prodded the sorrel, Elden pulled on the reins. Had the situation not been so fraught with peril, Nate would have enjoyed a hearty laugh.

The delay could well prove costly. Nate knew the two stalking Bloods would be pressing hard to overtake them, so he checked the opposite end of the defile often for sign of the two braves. Thankfully, neither appeared before the Leonards rode out. "Took you long enough," Nate couldn't help grousing.

Beads of perspiration lined Elden's glistening brow. He licked his lips and said softly, "I've never been so terrified in my whole life! Don't ever expect me to do anything like that again."

"You might surprise yourself," Nate said.

"What do you mean?"

"You'd be surprised at what you can do if it will make the difference between living and dying."

Elden snorted. "I really should be writing these pithy sayings of yours down for the benefit of posterity. When I'm safely back in New York, I can have them published and make my fortune."

A caustic retort was on the tip of Nate's tongue, but he forgot all about it when he spotted movement at the north entrance to the defile. The pair of warriors were coming and, predictably, coming fast. He'd hoped to put his plan into effect before they arrived to avoid more bloodshed, but Elden's reluctance had spoiled everything. "Our friends have shown up," he announced with a nod.

Elden took one look and cried, "Save us!"

"Save yourself," Nate responded, leaning over to give the sorrel a solid smack on the rump. The Indian horse broke into a gallop. Nate goaded his stallion into a gallop, but not away from the defile, *into* it. Traveling 30 feet, he sharply reined up, then drew his left flintlock.

Both Bloods held lances poised to throw. Blood lust marred their countenances. Neither, though, voiced the war whoops characteristic of braves everywhere, for an obvious reason.

Nate didn't want to do what had to be done. He'd much rather fight the warriors man-to-man, yet he was sensible enough to realize this wasn't the time for scruples. To save the greenhorns he must do the unthinkable.

The Bloods were a third of the way from the other opening when Nate lifted his arm as high as he could reach, cocked the pistol, and fired. In the confines of the defile the blast was nearly deafening, echoing and reechoing over and over. The Bloods instantly halted and cast troubled gazes upward. For all of 15 seconds nothing out of the ordinary transpired; then, with a staggering, rending crash, the snow on top of both high walls buckled and poured over the two crests.

Nate crammed the flintlock under his belt, wheeled the black stallion, and took flight. His enemies were doing the same. Body held low, he listened to the thunder far above him and swore the walls were shaking. The stallion apparently sensed the urgency because it fairly flew. A few small chunks of snow rained down, one striking him on the shoulder. He resisted the urge to look up and see how close he was to passing on to the great beyond. Ride! his mind screamed. Ride! Ride! Ride!

The opening swept to Nate's rear, but he still wasn't safe. There had been so much snow packed on the summit that some was bound to spill out the two ends of the defile. More clumps fell to the right and the left. Anxious to learn how far he must go to be in the clear, he twisted and beheld a sight that froze the blood in his veins.

A gargantuan cataract of snow was showering into the defile even as a tremendous backlash of billowy spray was shooting skyward. The next moment the opening itself was obliterated by a thundering alabaster cloud. From out of it spilled a tumbling wave 30 feet high.

Nate saw the torrent roaring toward him and rode as he had never ridden before. Vivid in his mind was the sensation of being buried alive by an icy cocoon, a sensation he never cared to experience again. The snow impeded the stallion terribly, and the roar grew to deafening proportions. Clods struck his back. Spray formed a mist around his head and shoulders. A solid ball of snow the size of his horse went hurling past. He was certain that he was going to be bowled over and he braced for the collision.

Then the roar abruptly diminished. The spray lessened to a few stray wisps. Nate looked and discovered the avalanche was losing momentum. The wave was now a series of white ripples, flowing slower and slower. He was safe.

Nate kept riding anyway until he caught up with the Leonards, who were waiting beside a stand of fir trees. As he came to a halt, Elden chortled.

"So the mighty mountain man is afraid of something after all! Who would have thought it?"

The Leonards were not prepared for what happened next. There was no forewarning. There were no grim threats or meaningless curses. Nate simply hauled off and punched Elden Leonard full on the mouth. Elden, venting a panicked squawk, toppled from the saddle like an ungainly goose taking a spill. "I've abided all of your insults I intend to," Nate declared. "The next time I won't pull my punch, and I'll use my butcher knife instead of my fist."

Elden lay on his back, gaping up at King. His bruised lips worked but no words came out.

Selena sat riveted in shock, her hands clutching her bosom. Suddenly she threw back her head and laughed in delight. "Someone should have done that years ago!" she exclaimed, and looked at Nate, anticipating he would join in her mirth. But he was already heading south.

"How can you say that?" Elden blubbered. "I've been mortally stricken by a barbarian and you find it humorous? Have you no compassion for your own flesh and blood?"

"You're not hurt, you simpleton," Selena responded, lowering her right arm toward him. "Now get up. I don't want to fall behind. I doubt our guide will wait for us in the mood he's in."

"Taken a fancy to him, have you?" Elden asked resentfully.

"What if I have?" Selena retorted.

Elden stared at the retreating broad shoulders of their protector. "I don't see what can interest you about a buckskin-clad buffoon."

"Haven't you been paying attention, dear brother? He has a cabin, doesn't he?"

"Yes. So?"

"So we need somewhere safe to hide out, don't we?"

The remark wasn't lost on Elden, whose pudgy features transformed into a devious, malignant mask. "How true, fair one," he said, and tittered gleefully. "Nate King will be repaid for his arrogance, and sooner than he could possibly imagine."

Chapter Five

Winona King was mending a torn buckskin shirt of her husband's when it occurred to her that their young son had been gone far too long. She glanced up at the door, which earlier she had opened a crack to admit fresh air, and saw that the light outside was fading. Sunset was not far off.

Setting the shirt, her buffalo bone needle, and her buffalo sinew thread on a table beside her, Winona rose from the chair and walked over to open the door. A gust of chill wind struck head-on, fanning her hip-length raven hair and causing goose flesh. "Zach!" she called out hopefully in perfectly accented English. "Time to come in." She waited a bit, then shouted again in the Shoshone tongue.

Only the groaning wind answered.

Troubled now, Winona turned and looked at her infant daughter, lying swathed in a thick blanket on the bed against the far wall. She had a decision to make: whether to take little Evelyn along or leave the baby there while she went searching for her son. Where a white mother might have been daunted at the idea of taking one so tiny out into the bone-numbing cold, Winona's hesitation was prompted by the thought of how helpless Evelyn would be if something unforeseen happened to her. The cold wasn't a factor at all, since from an early age Indian children were bred to tolerate conditions their white counterparts would have found intolerable.

Winona made up her mind. She went over and picked up the cradleboard lying next to the bed, then bundled Evelyn in it. Her cradleboard was similar to those used by the rest of the women in her tribe: narrow at the bottom, flared at the top, with a thick layer of buckskin on the outside and a soft leather lining inside to keep the baby snug and warm. Women in other tribes constructed theirs differently. The Utes, for instance, were known for making their cradleboards with the tops as wide as a woman's shoulders, while the Cheyennes did the exact opposite, making theirs so narrow the cradleboard fit between a woman's shoulder blades.

Donning her heavy robe, Winona next slipped the cradleboard onto her back, grabbed the flintlock rifle her husband had taught her to use, slung a leather bag containing a pouch of black powder and spare lead balls over her shoulder, and stepped out into the frosty air.

Down on the partially frozen lake nothing stirred. The usual ducks, geese, and brants were gone for the winter and wouldn't return again until spring. No other game was in sight either. The deer and elk were deep in the thickets, the smaller animals nestled in their burrows.

Winona longed to spot anything she could shoot for their next meal. A squirrel, a rabbit, she didn't care. Their food supply was critically low, and if Nate was

delayed for any reason, she might run out. That was
why Zach had gone off hunting, as he did every day.

The boy's tracks were easy to trail. Winona followed
them around the northeast corner of the cabin and into the
woods beyond. There was no sound other than the swish
of her moccasins through the deep snow, or the occasion-
al creak of one of the straps holding the cradleboard to
her back.

Since Zach had repeatedly been told by Nate never to
stray very far from the cabin when Nate wasn't home,
Winona expected to locate their offspring quickly. But
the boy had gone over a mile, to a meadow often used by
deer and elk when the weather was warmer, and stopped
behind a thicket. From there his tracks took Winona to
the rim of a ravine. She saw where he had knelt in the
snow, and glancing down into the ravine she saw why.
Fresh deer tracks told her that Zach had spotted a doe
and dropped to his knees to shoot. Crimson drops disclosed the doe had been hit. Instead of falling, the deer
had bounded on up the ravine with Zach in hot pursuit
along the rim.

This explained Zach's absence. Nate had taught the
boy to always go after wounded game, to never let an
animal suffer if it could be avoided. And sometimes, as
Winona knew, a stricken deer ran for miles before finally
expiring.

Hefting the flintlock, Winona hiked in her son's footsteps for over 15 minutes. The sun was halfway gone,
the shadows lengthening by the minute. Already the temperature was falling. She hoped the doe hadn't led the
boy too far afield.

The ravine opened out onto hilly terrain thick with
brush. Here Winona paused to scan the steadily dark-
ening highland and to call her son's name again. As
before, there was no response. Her anxiety mounting,

Winona forged on for over a mile. The sun had retired for the night and the last golden rays were rapidly fading when she came to the top of a hill and beheld a somber valley below, a valley she had never been in before and into which the doe had led Zach.

Quickening her pace, Winona carefully descended the slick slope and stopped at the bottom to get her bearings. The tracks bore due west. High firs, tightly clustered, prevented her from seeing more than a few dozen yards.

Evelyn gurgled softly as Winona tramped into the trees. The baby would need feeding soon, but Winona couldn't turn around and go back. Not until she found her son.

Suddenly, from off in the distance, came a faint, raspy snarl.

Winona ran, filled with dread that Zach had encountered a roving panther. Unlike grizzlies, which typically denned up for days at a time during the winter and were rarely seen, panthers prowled all year long. Ordinarily they gave humans a wide berth, but during the cold moons, when prey was most scarce, they became bolder, sometimes venturing into villages after horses or dogs. If one of the giant cats had come on Zach, hunger might have eclipsed its normal fear of man.

The snarl was repeated, a drawn-out cry of feline fury that enabled Winona to pinpoint the exact direction and alter her steps accordingly. As she neared the spot, she forced herself to slow down. To blunder onto the panther with a baby on her back might prove fatal to both of them. She rounded a trunk, then halted on hearing an irate young voice.

"Go away, you mangy, flea ridden, no-account cat! That deer is mine!"

The boy's outburst was greeted with another bestial snarl. Winona crept forward, her flintlock leveled at her waist. She spied a wide clearing ahead, and in it the cause of her son's anger. Padding round and round a lone fir tree that had taken root in the very middle of the open space was a huge lynx.

While not as massive as panthers, lynx were none-theless formidable in their own right, endowed as they were with powerful muscles and razor claws able to shred flesh as easily as a butcher knife shredded grass. Often close to four feet in length and weighing upwards of 45 pounds, they could hold their own against any oth-er creature in the mountains.

Winona saw this one stop and chew on the rear leg of the dead doe, which lay a few feet from the tree. She took another stride, setting her foot down silently. Should she so much as breathe loud, the cat would hear. Lynx were notorious for having outstanding hearing.

"Get away from there, you meat thief!" a flinty voice yelled. "You're blamed lucky I'm not a little older or I'd come down there and split your hairy skull with my tomahawk!"

Stopping, Winona peered into the fir. Her son was perched on a limb 20 feet up, his tomahawk clutched in his left hand. She wondered why he hadn't shot the lynx until she saw his rifle lying half buried in the snow near the deer.

"No worthless varmint is going to steal the kill of Stalking Coyote!" Zach blustered, referring to himself by his Shoshone name. "I'm the son of Grizzly Killer, you damn grimalkin!"

Winona had to grin. She watched the lynx slowly turn from the doe to the tree, then abruptly take a flying leap onto the trunk and begin clawing its way upward, making for her son. She darted into the open, pressed the rifle to her shoulder, and tried to get a bead. Intervening limbs thwarted her.

Zachary whooped for joy. Instead of cowering in fear, he waited until the lynx was almost upon him, then swung the tomahawk in a flashing arc. The sharp edge bit into the bole within inches of the lynx's face, forcing the cat to slant to one side. Hissing and spitting, the lynx swung a forepaw but missed. "Hold still, dang you!" the boy cried. He tried to bury his tomahawk in the cat a second time, to no avail.

Winona had shifted position for a better view of the lynx when it suddenly turned around and shot down out of the tree, jumping the final eight feet. As the cat alighted, it saw her and uttered a savage shriek. She aimed at its front shoulder, her finger beginning to close on the trigger, but in the blink of an eye the lynx spun and streaked off into the forest. Within moments it was gone.

"What in tarnation?" Zach blurted out, as yet oblivious of his mother's presence. "Afraid of me, are you!"

"I know I would be," Winona said.

"Ma!"

The boy came down out of the fir almost as rapidly as the lynx had done. Face aglow, he ran over and embraced her around the waist. "Am I ever glad to see you! I figured I'd be stuck in that dumb tree the whole night long." He stepped back and pointed proudly at the doe. "I got us meat! Lots of meat!"

"So I see," Winona responded. "You're a fine hunter."

Zachary's chest expanded and he beamed happily. "Wait until Pa hears. He says it takes real skill to bring down a deer at this time of year."

"Nate will be quite pleased," Winona agreed, her gaze on the rifle in the snow. "But I doubt that he will be as happy about the mistake you made."

"You know?" Zach responded, his tone betraying his astonishment. "How?"

"Why else didn't you shoot the lynx?" Winona inquired. She stepped to his gun and picked it up to confirm her deduction. "Tell me the whole story. And remember, I expect a straight tongue at all times."

The youngster's shoulders slumped. "I came on the doe by surprise and rushed my shot," he said. "I'm afraid I didn't drop it straight off, so I had to give chase." He stopped to slide the tomahawk under his belt. "Finally caught up when it was lying there dead. But the lynx had found it first."

"Go on," Winona prompted when the boy stopped.

Zach swallowed, then continued sheepishly, "I wasn't thinking straight. The sight of that cat eating our meat got me so riled I charged out of the woods and went to put a ball between its eyes."

"But?"

"But I'd plumb forgot to reload after I shot the doe."

"And what has your father told you about doing that?"

"A man should always reload as soon as he shoots so he's never, ever caught with an empty gun when he needs it the most," Zach quoted.

"I trust you have learned your lesson," Winona commented. "Many free trappers have been killed that way, and we would hate for the same thing to happen to you."

"I'm sorry, Ma. It won't happen again. Believe me."

"Tell me the rest."

Zach came over and squatted next to the doe. "Well, that ornery old lynx had run off a ways when I came at him. But then he turned and came slinking back. There wasn't no time for me to reload, so I just dropped the rifle and scrambled up the tree."

"Why didn't you take the rifle with you and reload up there?"

"I ..." Zach began, and looked at the ground, the rest of his words choked off by embarrassment.

"Let me take a guess," Winona said. "You were so rattled by the lynx coming after you that you panicked and dropped your gun so you could climb faster. Is this correct?"

The boy coughed. "Yes," he said, the word barely audible.

And that was the end of the matter. Winona set to reloading his rifle and said nothing more about his over-sights. She had made her point; that was enough. She knew that he knew he'd done wrong, and the next time he'd do better.

Indians never spanked or slapped their children, never belabored them endlessly over petty faults or flaws, no matter how severe the breach of conduct. Parents taught by example, and when mistakes had to be pointed out, it was done tactfully, with respect for the feelings of the child. This was how Winona had been reared and she did the same with Zach. Nate, to her dismay, didn't always agree with her methods, and there had been a few occasions when Zach had received a mild "tanning," as Nate called it, for especially bad behavior. The first time Winona had been horrified, certain their son would be emotionally ruined for life. To her amazement, though, the harsh discipline had actually proven effective, nor had it affected their son's love for them. Proving once again that sometimes the strange ways of the whites worked.

Once the rifle was ready, Winona gave it to her son and took hold of the doe by a rear leg. Zach imitated her example with the other leg, and together they head-ed homeward, dragging the deer behind them.

Night had claimed the Rockies. A myriad of stars twinkled in the heavens, and the full moon shone like an unblinking golden eye. To the northwest a wolf uttered a plaintive, wavering howl, and was answered shortly thereafter by another wolf to the southwest.

"I hope Pa won't be mad at me," Zach remarked lightheartedly.

"Over the rifle?" Winona responded.

"No, over me getting this deer. He went riding off up north to find game because he's had no luck close to home, and here I go and down this doe."

"I'm sure he'll forgive you," Winona said with a straight face.

"Do you figure he'll be back soon?"

"I hope so, but there is no telling. Knowing your father as I do, he'll keep hunting until he finds something. That could take a while."

The wind, as was invariably the case after sunset, intensified, rustling those pines not laden with snow. It brought with it faraway noises. Once, the hoot of an owl. Another time, the faint squeal of an animal being slain by a predator. And again, the yipping of a coyote.

Winona and Zach made steady progress. The doe was small, no strain to pull, and before too long they had climbed out of the valley and were crossing the brushy highland. Here the wind was stronger yet, plucking at their clothes with invisible fingers. They were almost to the ravine when they heard something that brought them both up short.

It was a guttural grunt.

"Ma?" Zach whispered nervously, staring at a hill to their left. "Is that what I think it is?"

"Yes. Hurry," Winona said, doing just that. She feared the scent of blood would attract the beast until she realized the wind was blowing from it to them and not the other way around. They were safe so long as the wind didn't shift.

"What do we do if it comes after us?" Zach asked.

"We do not let it take the doe."

"Even if it's a big one?"

"We do not let it take the doe," Winona repeated sternly. They needed fresh meat in order to survive; she needed meat in order to stay healthy and keep producing the milk Evelyn required. She'd resist with all her might no matter how big the brute might be.

In tense silence they hastened homeward, moving at twice the speed. Their breathing became labored. Soon they began to tire, not from the weight of the doe, but from the sustained exertion of having hauled the carcass over a mile. The forest swallowed them again, veiling them in murky shadow.

Although Winona was filled with apprehension, she resolutely refused to let her feelings show, to betray her anxiety to her son. Since childhood she had been raised to be level-headed in the face of danger, to confront adversity without flinching. Shoshone women took great pride in being as courageous as their men, in being a credit to their families and their people, and Winona was no exception. She would do what must be done.

Because the trees blocked off nearly all the moonlight, Winona and Zach had to pick their way carefully, avoiding logs and whatever else might bar their path. Minutes had gone by with only the wind for company, and Winona began to think they had outdistanced the creature they had heard, when another grunt let her know the thing was still out there and much closer than it had been the first time they heard it.

"It's following us, Ma," Zach said.

"Yes," Winona responded, and tried to go even faster, but the deep snow clung to her legs, slowing her.

Head lowered, she plodded onward. Giving up was out of the question. However, she might have to stop shortly whether she wanted to or not. Her son's loud breaths and stooped posture were signs he was near the limits of his endurance although he was gamely refusing to quit.

Another minute dragged by. Winona noticed the darkness deepen. She figured the moon had gone behind a drifting cloud, yet when she idly glanced at the sky, there it was in all its gleaming glory. The reason the light had dimmed even more was because a row of tall pines 20 feet above her now shut out nearly all the moonlight. With a start she realized they had blundered into the ravine instead of going around it.

The surprise brought Winona to a stop. She glanced around and saw they were at least a dozen yards from the opening. Since she didn't care to be caught in so confined a space by the hulking brute trailing them, she started to turn, to go back out and swing to the south.

From the woods adjacent to the ravine mouth rose a low, rumbling growl.

"Ma?" Zach asked uncertainly. He sensed the worry in his mother and knew something was wrong although he didn't know exactly what. They were in the ravine, yes, but he mistakenly believed his mother had steered them into it deliberately so they could make better time since the snow wasn't quite as deep.

"Don't look back," Winona told him, bending her shoulders to their mutual effort. The high walls shut off the groaning of the wind, and now the only sounds were those they made themselves and the scraping of the deer. She thought of her lovely new daughter and wondered if she had made a mistake in not leaving the child in the cabin. A slow death by starvation might be preferable to the violence the beast would wreak on them if it elected to contest their ownership of the doe.

"Look, Ma!" Zach abruptly exclaimed, pointing at the south rim.

An enormous black shape was moving along the top of the ravine wall about 30 feet to their rear, a veritable walking mountain, so big its shoulders rose half as high as some of the pines.

"We must reach the end of the ravine before it does," Winona declared. She did not add that if they didn't, they would be trapped. Redoubling her pace, she avoided a boulder and nearly fell when the sole of her left moccasin came down on a slippery flat stone.

"Pa says never to show them any fear," Zach remarked between puffs. "They can smell it."

"Let us hope this one has a cold," Winona joked to ease the nervousness her son's tone betrayed.

"Why isn't it sleeping in a den somewhere?" Zach asked irately. "That's what I'd like to know."

"They venture out now and then during the colder moons," Winona reminded him. "It is just our luck this one picked tonight."

Somberly they forged onward. From above them came the loud sound of regular wheezing breaths and the dull thud of heavy footfalls. Snow slid over the crest every so often. The brute was not even trying to move stealthily.

"If it charges, Ma, you take Evelyn and head for the cabin. I'll hold it off," Zach declared.

"You will do no such thing. I will not have you risking your life."

"What about your life? What about the baby?"

Winona looked at her son, about to admonish him for arguing with her at such a time, when the sight of him struggling so valiantly to pull the doe stilled her tongue. She had to remember that he was almost ten now, and while he was years away from becoming a full-fledged warrior, he wasn't a helpless, inexperienced child any longer.

Among the Shoshones, boys were taught the arts of manhood at an early age, and she had insisted on doing the same with Zach. She and Nate had spent countless hours teaching their son the basics of wilderness survival. Under Nate's tutelage Zach had learned to hunt, track, and butcher game. Under Winona's guidance the boy had learned to cook, to find herbs and edible plants in season, and to cure and tan hides.

As Zach's knowledge had grown, so had his responsibilities around the cabin. Each member of their family had specific chores to do daily, and Zach had been doing his faithfully, without complaint, since he was four. That was as it should be, as it was done among the Shoshones.

But back in the States, Nate had told Winona, conditions were different. More often than not, boys back there were pampered by their parents during their early years and never taught more than how to eat, dress themselves, and play. The children were seldom given jobs to do; their parents did it all for them. The children were spoiled to the core, as Nate had put it, and as a result they grew into temperamental, selfish adults who thought the world owed them everything.

Winona had found the white practice bewildering, since it was bound to bring about the ruin of both the children and their parents, but it did go a long way toward explaining much of the inexplicable behavior and attitudes demonstrated by the whites at times.

The next moment Winona's reverie was shattered by a yelp from her son, and glancing up, she saw they were near the end of the ravine. She also saw something that made her go rigid with misgiving, for barring the mouth of the ravine was the thing that had been following them: a huge grizzly bear.

Chapter Six

Many miles to the north, Nate King lay on his back under his blankets beside the dying fire and pursed his lips in self-reproach. He had been trying to get to sleep for some time with no success. Whether because of the excitement he felt at the prospect of being reunited with his loved ones sometime during the next day or the reservations he had about taking the Leonards to his cabin, he was too agitated to sleep.

Thinking that a short stroll would clear his head and calm him down, Nate threw the blankets off, grabbed his Hawken, and walked a few yards to the horses. He made certain the sorrel was securely tethered, since to lose it now would result in a two-day delay, or more. Then, stepping to the west side of the clearing in which they had made camp, he leaned against a tree and respectfully regarded the night sky. His soul never ceased to thrill to the celestial spectacle afforded by the countless stars, more stars than he could ever recall seeing back in New York. Perhaps, he often reasoned, the elevation was responsible. New York City was virtually at sea level, while the mountain valleys were often more than a mile high. Instead of being in some far-off galaxy, the stars seemed to be suspended just out of reach of his fingertips.

Had Nate been able, he would have plucked one of the sparkling dots of light down and made a wish on it, a fervent wish that all would go well once he arrived home. He lacked solid reasons for believing there would be trouble, yet he couldn't shake a persistent feeling that he was making a mistake. This in itself was disturbing, especially since the Leonards were treating him so nicely, even Elden.

The big change had first been evident shortly after the incident at the defile. Elden had become a paragon of courtesy, never once sassing Nate or whining. Then, that evening, Elden had volunteered to water their horses at a nearby spring. It was as if the man had undergone some sort of mysterious change that had transformed him into a whole new person. Nate didn't know what to make of it.

Selena was another matter. On more than one occasion Nate had caught her in the act of studying him. Always she had smiled sweetly and acted as if nothing out of the ordinary was taking place, but each time there had been an odd quality about her gaze that troubled him. He'd tried convincing himself he was reading something into her attitude that wasn't there, yet it still upset him.

"I must be touched in the head," Nate said softly to himself, and grinned.

"I wouldn't say that."

The voice was so close behind Nate that he inadvertently jumped, then whirled. Selena Leonard stood a few feet away, grinning coyly.

"My apologies. I didn't mean to startle you."

"I was deep in thought," Nate said while marveling at how quietly she had approached. Rarely did anyone take him by surprise anymore, and for a rank greenhorn to do it was unsettling. "I thought you'd be sound asleep by now," he added to change the subject.

Selena moved nearer and folded her arms across her bosom. "I tried. But after all that has happened to us, I'm afraid I don't sleep as soundly as I used to."

"Give yourself time. You've been through a lot."

"If you only knew," Selena said enigmatically. She stared upward, her smooth features flawless in the lunar glow. "These mountains of yours certainly are beautiful."

"That they are," Nate wholeheartedly agreed. "It's another reason I decided to stay here instead of returning to civilization. A grimy chimney is a poor substitute for a mountain. And a city park is no comparison to the wide open spaces of the Rockies and the prairie."

"Point well taken," Selena said. "You have the heart of a romantic, I see."

"I just read a lot of Cooper when I was younger," Nate said lamely.

"James Fenimore Cooper? You like him also?" Selena gave a soft laugh. "What a remarkable coincidence. He's one of my favorite writers, has been ever since I read *The Pioneers*."

"The one I like the most is *The Last of the Mohicans*," Nate divulged, and almost took a step backward when she snatched his hand happily.

"Mine too!" Selena exclaimed. "How extraordinary! We must have more in common than would be apparent or we wouldn't have similar literary tastes. I wonder what else we both like."

"I have no idea," Nate said. He was too polite to note that she was making a bigger fuss over Cooper than was warranted. "But I would doubt we have very much in common. Men who live here for very long change in ways you couldn't possibly appreciate."

"Are you referring to all those quaint words you use now and then, like 'chawing' and what have you?"

"That's part of it," Nate grinned. "Mountanee men do have a colorful way of talking, and once a man gets the habit it's hard to break." He nodded at a white peak close by. "But I meant a different kind of change, one that takes place deep inside. Live in these mountains long enough and you'll never look at the world the same way again."

"How interesting. Tell me more."

Nate suddenly realized she still held his hand. He disengaged it gently and placed it behind him, bracing his palm against the tree trunk. "I don't rightly know if I can do it justice with words," he said. "There are some things in life a person has to experience to know what they're really like."

"I'd like to learn," Selena said, and gave a sigh that caused the top of her dress to swell dramatically. "One of the reasons we came west was our desire to see new sights, to experience what few others ever had."

Nate tried to conceive of Elden being invested with the spirit of curiosity and adventure, and couldn't.

"Would you care to hear our story?" Selena asked.

"If you care to tell it."

"To be honest, I'm surprised you haven't inquired before this," Selena said. "Surely you've wanted to know?"

"Whether I did or didn't doesn't count," Nate replied. "Out here folks mind their own business. It's considered downright rude to go sticking your nose into the personal lives of others unless someone offers up information."

"What an admirable custom," Selena said. She turned to survey the forest to the south so her back was to him as she said, "Well, allow me to explain. My brother and I come from a well-to-do family. Neither of us has ever had to work for a living, which you might think would be a blessing, but it isn't." She paused. "With so much free time on our hands, we can never find enough to do. We spend most of our days bored to death. As a result, we're always ready to see new sights, to know new thrills."

"Which is what brought you from New York," Nate said when she stopped.

"Yes. We'd read and heard so much about the frontier, we decided we should pay it a visit and see if it was as exciting as everyone told us it would be."

"At times it can be a little *too* exciting if a body isn't real careful."

"Truer words were never spoken. We hired boatmen to take us up the Mississippi to the Missouri, and from there we traveled deep into the plains. We fished, hunted buffalo and antelope, and generally had a fine time." Her voice dropped. "Then came the day of the storm."

"What happened?"

"It was the most terrifying spectacle I have ever witnessed," Selena said gravely. "There we were, hiking on the prairie after buffalo, when out of the west swept enormous black storm clouds. They were on us before we could get back to the boats. There was no place to hide, no place to run. Somehow we became separated from our guides." She clasped her arms together and shuddered.

"If you'd rather not talk about it," Nate said to be polite.

"I'm all right," Selena assured him. "I'd just never seen a storm like that one. The rain was so heavy we couldn't see more than a few feet in front of our faces. The wind bowled us over several times. And the lightning! It struck all around us without letup for over an hour. There was nothing Elden and I could do except curl up in the high grass and hope for the best." Selena turned. "It was a miracle we weren't killed. When the storm moved on, we got up and called out to our guides but they didn't answer."

"Why not? You couldn't have drifted that far apart."

"We hadn't," Selena said. "We didn't understand their silence either until Elden found their bodies." The corners of her mouth twitched. "A bolt of lightning had hit right between them and killed them both instantly." She looked into his eyes. "Have you ever seen a man charred to a crisp, his flesh blistered and black, his hair and clothes all burned off, his face like something out of a madman's nightmare? It was utterly horrible."

"I can imagine it would be."

"We had nothing to bury them with. There was nothing we could do but head back to the river. But we hadn't gone far when a group of riders appeared on the horizon. None of our party had horses, but we had been told there were trappers in the area who did."

"So you figured they were friendly," Nate said.

"Yes. We yelled and jumped up and down to attract their attention. The next thing we knew, we were surrounded by a pack of screaming fiends. The Bloods, you called them. They tied our hands, threw us on two of their horses, and headed westward. We'd still be in their clutches if not for you." Selena smiled gratefully.

"I'm glad I could help," Nate said. He stifled a yawn and realized he was now tired enough to fall asleep. Straightening, he had in mind suggesting they both turn in so they would be well refreshed come morning, when the discrepancy in her account rooted him in place. "Didn't you just tell me the Bloods put you on two of their own horses?" he asked.

Selena seemed to tense slightly. "Yes. Why?"

"That's mighty strange. You see, two of those horses were shod, and I figured they must have belonged to Elden and you."

"You mean to say Indians don't shoe their mounts?"

Nate laughed. "They sure don't. Few of the tribes know anything about working with metal. That's why they like to trade with the whites so much, to get all the things they can't make themselves."

"I didn't know," Selena said almost in a whisper. Then she glanced up and grinned self-consciously. "We learn something new every day, don't we?" She paused. "As for the horses, all I can tell you is what happened. The Bloods had two extra mounts with them, and they were the animals we were put on. I have no idea where the savages obtained them. Is it important?"

"Not really. They had to have stolen them from some other whites," Nate said.

"I hope they didn't kill anyone doing it."

"Did you see any of the warriors carrying fresh scalps tied to their lances or around their waists?" Nate asked.

"No."

"It's odd they—" Suddenly Selena Leonard unexpectedly hurled herself at him and wrapped her arms around his neck. Before he could organize his wits, she was clinging to him and sobbing pathetically. Her moist tears trickled down his skin, her warm breath fanned his throat. "Selena?" he said, his voice unusually hoarse, but she ignored him and kept on crying. Not wishing to be rude, he simply stood there and let her express the grief that had built up inside her. She was pressed tight against him, and he could feel her heaving bosom. After a while, he was disconcerted to find his body growing warm and his cheeks flushed. "Selena?" he repeated rather gruffly.

"Yes?" she answered, and sniffled loudly.

"I think you should get ahold of yourself," Nate advised.

"I'm sorry." Selena pulled back and dabbed at her face with a sleeve. "It's just that I've been through so much, and Elden hasn't been much help."

"You have nothing to be sorry for," Nate said. "I understand completely." He gave her shoulder a squeeze. "Now why don't we turn in? A good night's rest is just what we both need."

"Whatever you want, Nate," Selena said throatily. "Whatever you want."

Winona King saw the ominous bulk of the menacing grizzly move toward her and she released the leg of the doe, raised her flintlock, and took two steps to the left to put herself between the bear and her son. She pulled back the hammer and tried to take hurried aim, but the inky murk at the bottom of the ravine prevented her from telling exactly where to shoot to strike a vital organ. As a result, she hesitated, unwilling to risk merely angering the beast.

Zach appeared at her side, his own rifle elevated. "We'll fight it together, Ma," he declared.

"I want you to run," Winona said.

"The son of Grizzly Killer doesn't turn tail from a dumb old bear."

Pride welled up in Winona's heart. She saw the grizzly stop a dozen feet away and heard its heavy breathing. There wasn't enough space in the ravine for them to try and go around it, and retreating might provoke a charge.

All she could do was stand there and wait for the bear to make up its mind whether to attack or not. If it did, they'd each be able to get off a single shot, and if neither ball proved fatal, the brute would rip them to pieces in a mad rage.

"Try and keep it off us," Zach said urgently. "I have an idea."

"What?" Winona asked, but the boy was gone, darting out of sight behind her. There was a thud, then a whole flurry of blows, as if Zach was beating the deer carcass. She would have glanced around to see what he was doing, only the grizzly suddenly advanced a few feet. Winona perceived the outline of its massive head, swinging ponderously from side to side, and she listened to it sniffing the air. Sighting down the flintlock, she tried to locate one of its eyes.

"Almost done," Zach called out.

Bothered by the flurry of movement and sound, the grizzly growled, then suddenly reared back and rose onto its hind legs.

Winona had to tilt her head back to see the top of the monster. Its teeth shone dully in the darkness, and she thought she saw its tongue dart out and in. Pointing the barrel at a spot between the teeth, she prepared to fire if the bear took a single step further. It made no sinister gestures, however, and only stood there sniffing.

"Got it, Ma!" Zach cried, dashing around. In his left hand he held his butcher knife, in his right a haunch off the doe. He took a stride and waved the piece overhead. "Here you go, bear! This is what you want!" Then, drawing back his right arm, he hurled the haunch as far as he could. It landed with a thud to the left of the grizzly. "Let's pray this works," he said.

The clever ruse impressed Winona. She wondered why she hadn't thought of it, and she watched with bated breath as the beast dropped onto all fours again and turned to examine the haunch. Everything depended on what the grizzly did next.

Grunting and rumbling, the bear ran its nose up and down the meat. It shifted once to regard them balefully, then it took the haunch in its iron jaws, spun almost gracefully for a creature so gigantic, and bounded off, slanting to the right once it was out of the ravine. Brush crackled and snapped as the grizzly plowed into the forest. Within moments the noise of its passage had faded to silence.

"There is no time to waste," Winona said, laying hold of the doe. "The bear might come back for more."

"I didn't know what else to do," Zach said. He grabbed a leg and helped her drag the remainder of the body off. "Pa always says if you can't outfight an enemy, you should outsmart him."

"You did fine," Winona said, her ears pricked to catch the faintest sounds. When grizzlies wanted to, they could move as silently as the wind. She must stay vigilant all the way back to their cabin or risk being set upon before she could so much as lift her rifle.

Neither of them spoke. Resolve lining their features, they refused to stop, not even when the cabin loomed out of the night before them. Winona went straight to the door and threw it open. With Zach's assistance, she carried the carcass inside and placed it on the wooden counter. Lighting a lantern was her next chore. Then, moving swiftly, she slipped the cradleboard off of her shoulders so she could check on her daughter.

Evelyn was asleep, her dainty hands curled under her pointed chin, none the worse for wear for having been out in the cold for hours.

Winona placed her daughter on the bed. Zach, without being bidden, was kindling a stack of wood in the fireplace. She went over and draped a hand on his arm. "There was no time to say more back in the ravine, but I want you to know that what you did was very brave and very wise, my son. Your father will be happy to hear. And I will tell the story around the campfires of our people so the Shoshones will know our son is already well on his way to being a mighty warrior."

The boy lit up like a miniature sun. "There's no need to do that, Ma," he said, but his tone belied the statement.

"Nonsense. The other mothers are always boasting about their children. I can do no less for mine." Grinning, Winona reclaimed her rifle. "I will see how the horses are doing and be right back."

"Watch out for that darn bear."

The reminder was unnecessary, since the grizzly was uppermost on Winona's mind. She dreaded the thought of the brute trailing them home and later on possibly tearing into the pen or trying to break inside the cabin. Nor were her fears farfetched. Grizzlies had been known to enter cabins and lodges before, usually with disastrous results for the occupants. Once, many winters ago, a particularly vicious bear that had plagued her tribe for many moons tore through the side of a lodge in the middle of the night and made off with a little girl who had been sleeping in her mother's arms. The mother's head had been ripped off.

So Winona had the flintlock cocked as she stepped to the southeast corner of the structure and scanned the enclosure Nate had built for their horses. All the animals were present except Nate's stallion. To be safe, she made a complete circuit of the pen and the cabin, pausing often to attune her mind to the rhythm of the woodland. All she heard was the sighing of the wind, the rustling of trees. The grizzly, evidently, was gone.

Flames were crackling in the hearth when Winona entered, closed the door behind her, and set in place the heavy wooden bar designed to keep out unwanted intruders. She pulled down the leather flap covering the expensive glass pane Nate had installed in the window just for her benefit, then stripped off her robe and hung it on a peg on the wall.

Zach was staring intently into the fire, immersed in reflection. He heard her approach and turned. "Anything?"

"We're safe. If the bear should come around, the horses will let us know."

"Too bad Blaze isn't here," Zach said, referring to the gray wolf cub he had found wandering in a blizzard over a year ago and raised as a pet. Initially the cub had never strayed from Zach's side, but the more it had grown, the more independent it had become, and now it spent two out of every three days off in the wilderness.

"Your father thinks Blaze has found a pack to run with," Winona commented. She walked to the bed and smiled in delight when she saw Evelyn awake and studying her. "My little precious," she said, lifting the child out of the cradleboard. "If you knew what you had been through tonight, your hair would turn gray."

Evelyn cooed and wagged her chubby arms.

"Are you hungry?" Winona asked, moving to a chair near the fireplace. She made herself comfortable and slipped the top of her loose-fitting buckskin dress over her shoulder, exposing her right breast. Evelyn needed no coaxing and was soon sucking greedily.

"What does that feel like, Ma?"

Winona saw a look of entranced awe on her son's face, and grinned. "It feels—nice."

"I sure am glad I wasn't born female."

"Why is that?"

"I wouldn't want anyone slurping on me the way she does, getting slobber all over everything. And after hearing about how babies are born, I don't know if I could handle having something squirming around inside of me."

"Men," Winona said.

"What?"

"Indian or white, they are all alike." Winona smiled. "Trust me, my son. Giving birth is the most wonderful joy a woman can know. Yes, there is some pain. But to hold new life in your hands, life that came from inside you, that you nurtured and carried for nine long moons, is an experience too wonderful for words."

"If you say so."

"We will see if you change your attitude after you have taken a wife and had a child of your own," Winona said.

"I doubt I . . ." Zach responded, falling quiet of a sudden as he leaped erect and swung toward the door, his hand falling to his butcher knife.

Winona twisted in her chair, hearing the same thing he did.

Something was sniffing at the door.

Chapter Seven

When Nate King rode over the crest of a high ridge to the north of the secluded valley in which his home was located and saw the quaint cabin bathed in the light of the morning sun, he smiled and clucked the stallion into a brisk walk. He couldn't wait to see his wife and children again. Unlike many free trappers who could go off into the wilderness for weeks on end and not be at all upset about being separated from their loved ones, Nate missed his family more the longer he was away from them. Some of his friends had joked about his devotion, claiming he was soft in the heart, but he ignored them. To his way of thinking his family came first and foremost at all times.

The remote valley was as tranquil as ever. A few pillowy clouds floated on high through the vivid blue sky. The wind had temporarily died, and the surface of the lake was as smooth as fine china.

As Nate wound lower among the pines, he took note of the fact there was no smoke curling from the chimney. That made him a little uneasy, since he knew Winona would keep the fire going almost constantly to keep the baby from developing the chills. Perhaps, he speculated, she was off chopping wood or maybe out after small game.

Once on the flat valley floor Nate brought the stallion to a trot. Snow flew from under its pounding hoofs as he crossed a meadow and plunged into more trees. Behind him came the Leonards, Selena riding in the front this time and Elden holding fast to her waist.

"Did you build the cabin yourself?" she now inquired.

"My Uncle Zeke did," Nate answered. "I added a stone fireplace and a few other touches to make it more comfortable for us."

"Doesn't your family miss having neighbors?"

"We do have neighbors."

Selena scanned the valley from end to end. "Where?"

"Friends of ours, the McNairs, live about twenty-five miles away. We visit them or they visit us every couple of months and we all have a fine old time." Nate went around a log. "They're the nearest ones, but there are a few other trappers living in this particular mountain range."

"I don't see how you can stand it being so crowded," Elden interjected.

Nate swung to the southeast to approach the cabin from the front. From several hundred yards off he saw the front door hanging wide open, and immediately he urged the black stallion into a gallop.

"What is your hurry?" Selena called out.

Apprehension was the cause, but Nate was in too much of a hurry to waste breath telling her. His concern stemmed from his long-running dispute with the

Utes over his right to live where he pleased. The valley happened to lie at the extreme northeast corner of territory the Utes claimed, and since they had no desire to share, particularly with whites, they had repeatedly tried to kill him. Only the hand of Providence had spared him and his family from their traps and ambushes so far.

Nate sometimes reflected that he was merely being stubborn; the Rockies were vast and there were bound to be other spots which would appeal to him as much as his cherished valley. Yet he stayed on anyway. Perhaps, he often reasoned, it had something to do with his Uncle Zeke, who had staked out this valley years ago, and to whom Nate had become quite attached before Zeke was killed by a Kiowa warrior. The valley, and specifically the cabin, held a sentimental attachment he was reluctant to sever.

As Nate neared his home he cocked the Hawken. All the horses appeared to be in the corral, but there was still no sign of his wife or his son. He was out of the saddle before the stallion came to a complete stop. Dashing toward the doorway, he saw a vague shape appear out of the interior, and he drew up short, leveling his rifle. "You!" he blurted out.

Framed in the entrance was a majestic wolf with a wide white mark on its hairy chest. Triangular ears peaked, black nose twitching, it regarded him coolly for a moment, then advanced with its bushy tail wagging and its lips curled back in a welcoming smile.

"Where are they, Blaze?" Nate asked as he absently rubbed the wolf under the chin. "Take me to Zach and Winona."

At the mention of the boy's name, the wolf turned and padded around the corner. Nate followed, casting a look back as the Leonards rode up. "Stay here!" he directed, and was gone before either of them could voice an objection or a query.

Blaze seemed to know exactly where to go. At a slow lope the wolf headed through the forest, to the southwest.

Nate's ears told him why long before his eyes did. The dull thud of an ax biting into wood caused relief to flood through him. When, a minute later, he saw them in a clearing ahead, he slowed and savored the sight.

Winona, the cradleboard strapped to her back, stood to one side of a dead pine watching her son wield the heavy ax. Zach was doing his best, struggling each time he threw his entire body into a swing. Neither of them paid much attention when Blaze bounded up.

Smiling to himself, Nate crept silently up behind his wife. He could barely contain his mirth as he jabbed her in the side and vented a bloodthirsty screech. His intent had been to make her jump, but he had failed to take her Shoshone heritage into account. Instead of being spooked, as most any white woman would have been, Winona whirled, swinging her flintlock like a club. Had Nate not been holding one arm at chest height, he would have lost some teeth. As it was, the blow sent him stumbling backward, his forearm and face lanced with pain. He tripped over his own feet, then fell onto his back and lay there in the snow, dazed.

"Husband!" Winona squealed. "I thought I was being attacked!"

Dimly, Nate realized someone was kneeling at his side and felt cool fingers on his sore mouth. Another hand squeezed his arm to determine if any bones were broken. Through a haze he beheld the most beautiful face in creation hovering above him, and he muttered, "Lord, you're magnificent."

"Don't talk," Winona said. "Your lip is split."

"Is that all? It feels like my head."

"Whatever possessed you to do such a thing? I might have shot you by mistake."

"It was my idea of a joke," Nate explained. "White people do it to each other all the time."

"Do many of them live?"

Hearty laughter added insult to the indignity, and Nate twisted to see his son doubled over in uncontrollable mirth. "Do you always delight in the misery of others, young man?"

"No, Pa," Zach replied between guffaws. "But you should have seen the look on your face when Ma walloped you! I've never seen anyone so surprised in all my born days."

"Hmmmmph," Nate responded for lack of a wittier response. Sitting up, he rubbed his jaw and touched his lips. A speck of blood decorated his fingertip when he drew his hand away. "I'd best get some cold water on this before my mouth swells up." He girded his legs to rise when the tranquility was shattered by a scream of sheer terror coming from the direction of the cabin. Nate took one look around the clearing and exclaimed, "Blaze!" Shoving erect, he shut out the throbbing in his forehead and sped off.

"Who was that?" Winona yelled, sprinting after him.

"Company," Nate answered. Another scream spurred him to greater speed. Blaze was friendly toward him and his family, but a typical wild wolf where strangers were concerned. He envisioned one of the Leonards taking a stick to the animal and having a hand ripped off before he could get there.

Through the evergreens and around the cabin Nate ran. The scream had ended, and he didn't quite know what he would find, but certainly never expected to find what he did: Selena, laughing softly, perched on the bottom limb of a tree, with her brother sprawled in an unconscious heap on the ground underneath her and Blaze astride Elden's chest, licking the man's face. "What in the world?" Nate declared.

Blaze looked up, gave Elden a final lick, and padded off into the brush.

"My apologies," Nate said, advancing. "The wolf is a pet, when it wants to be. Are you all right?"

"Never better," Selena said. "We didn't know if it would be friendly or not, and when I saw it coming at us I'm afraid I let out a yell." She cautiously lowered herself to the ground. "We ran for this tree, but poor Elden passed out. Then the wolf jumped on top of him." She shrugged. "I thought he was doomed and screamed again. I'm terribly sorry for being so weak."

"You did what was to be expected," Nate said, squatting beside Elden. He gave the man's cheek a light slap. Elden groaned and his eyelids fluttered but he didn't come around. "Did he hit his head on anything?"

"No, I don't think—" Selena began, and gave a tiny gasp.

Shifting, Nate saw her gaping at Winona and Zach, both of whom were approaching. His wife, he deduced, must have waited for the boy to catch up. Introductions were in order so he rose and made them.

"*This* is your family?" Selena said in amazement. She beamed, giggled girlishly, then impulsively took a step and warmly embraced a surprised Winona. "Mrs. King! You have no idea what a pleasure this is."

"I am pleased to meet you, Miss Leonard."

"My word!" Selena said, drawing back. "You speak better English than I do."

"I have had a good teacher," Winona said, stepping to Nate's side and taking his hand in hers.

The corners of Selena's eyes crinkled. "Evidently,"

she said sweetly. Then: "I hope you don't mind us inconveniencing you in this fashion. Your husband saved us from a band of Bloods, and he promised we'd be able to stay here a few days, then go on to Fort Laramie."

"We are delighted to have you," Winona assured her, and motioned at the cabin. "In a short while my son will have a fire going, so come inside and make yourself comfortable."

"I'd be glad to."

Nate watched the two of them stroll in, pleased they seemed to be getting along so well together. Bending down, he hooked his hands under Elden's shoulder and hoisted the heavyset man to a sitting posture.

"What?" Elden mumbled, the jostling reviving him at last. His eyes snapped open and he abruptly let out a squeal, waving his arms violently as if warding off a monster.

"You're safe," Nate said, holding tight. "The wolf is gone."

"King?" Elden looked around. "Thank goodness! Did you scare it off? You should have seen the horrid teeth on the thing!" Opening his mouth to say more, he caught sight of Zach and blurted out, "Say, who's the Indian brat?"

"My son," Nate answered harshly, surging upright. So quickly did he move that gravity spilled Elden back to the ground. "And if you value your health, you'll never, ever speak about him that way again."

"I didn't mean nothing by it," Elden said. "Honest."

"Sure you didn't," Nate responded. Beckoning Zach, he took the two horses to the pen and stripped his saddle off the stallion while explaining the circumstances that had resulted in having the pair of greenhorns as guests.

"I know you say we should try to like everyone," Zach commented when his father was done, "but I have to be honest with you, Pa. I don't think much of that Mr. Leonard and I hardly know the man."

"You're not to blame," Nate said. "I don't think much of him either, and I know him fairly well."

Raucous laughter rang in the cabin as the two of them entered. Selena and Elden were seated on chairs by the fire, sipping tea as they conversed with Winona. All three were having a grand time.

"There you are!" Selena exclaimed. "Join us. Your charming wife has been entertaining us with delightful stories about frontier life."

Elden lowered his tin cup. "I hope you're not going to hold a grudge over that stupid remark I made when I came to. I've already admitted what I did to your wife and told her I was sorry."

"A dozen times," Winona said.

"How nice," Nate said flatly. Still simmering over the insult to his son, he leaned the Hawken against the wall and deposited his saddle in a corner. From a bucket on the corner he filled a ladle with water to slake his thirst, and as he dropped the ladle back in he observed that the bucket was almost empty. "Be back in a bit," he declared, grasping the handle.

"Where are you going?" Elden asked.

"To the lake," Nate replied.

"I could use some fresh air," Elden said, passing his tea to his sister. "Mind if I tag along?"

"Suit yourself," Nate replied, striding out into the brilliant sunshine. He didn't wait for the greenhorn, but hiked eastward, the bucket swinging in his right hand.

"Hold on!" Elden said, puffing up beside him. "I know you're mad at me, but at least give me a chance to redeem myself in your eyes."

"Who's mad?" Nate rasped defensively.

"Come now, King. I'm not a complete idiot," Elden

said affably. "If someone called my son a brat, I know I'd be furious enough to eat nails." He extended his hands, palms outward. "What can I say that will justify it? I'll tell you. There is nothing I can say. All I can do is throw myself on my knees and beg your forgiveness."

Nate was utterly astonished when, a second later, Leonard did exactly that, right in his path. He halted and gazed down at the man's earnest features. "Don't," he declared. "A man never begs."

"Mountain men, perhaps. But I'm a New Yorker," Elden said. "Hell, you saw me. I faint sometimes when my life is endangered. I ask you. What sort of *man* does that?"

"It happens," Nate said, although in truth he had never heard of any male over the age of ten being so afflicted. Bending, he gripped Leonard by the shoulders and pulled him to his feet. "There's no need to demean yourself."

"But I want you to believe me when I say I'm truly sorry."

"I do."

"Really, or are you just saying that to make me feel better?" Elden grasped the trapper's wrist. "This is important to me. I like you, King, and I don't want any ill will between us. Especially since you've so graciously offered to take us in."

Seldom had Nate encountered two people so glibly persuasive as the Leonards. They had a knack for using words to get their way, and now, while his resentment of Elden had not diminished a whit, he found himself saying, "There are no hard feelings. You can rest easy."

"Thank you," Elden said, pumping Nate's arm vigorously. "I'm hoping the two of us can be friends by the time this is over."

"Anything is possible," Nate allowed. Extricating his arm from Leonard's unexpectedly strong grip, he continued along the path toward the lake. So many times had one or the other of his family gone for water since the snow fell that a well-worn rut marked the trail plainly. He was too deep in thought, though, to notice this or anything else about his surroundings.

Nate was extremely annoyed at himself for saying things he didn't mean. He had always taken inordinate pride in his truthfulness; he shunned lying like preachers shunned sin. If a thing wasn't so, he'd never deny it. Yet here he was, telling the simple-minded greenhorn that he harbored no ill will when he actually did. He disliked Elden intensely. And his feelings were nurtured by more than Leonard's previous behavior. There was something about the man that rankled Nate, an indefinable quality that made Nate want to haul off and punch Elden in the face for no other reason than the man existed.

This in itself was annoying. Nate considered himself a logical man. Why, then, did he have this illogical attitude toward Elden? Especially since Leonard was being straightforward with him? It wasn't every day he met a man willing to admit to being a coward and a bit of a fool.

Behind the trapper, Elden took a deep breath and said, "These mountains of yours certainly are invigorating! The air is so fresh it makes you tingle! And it's so clear you can see for miles and miles."

"Except on cloudy days," Nate said.

"I bet this climate promotes one's health," Elden said. "Why, I haven't been so full of vigor and vim since I was a child. A few weeks of this and I'll be a completely new person."

Nate envisioned being cooped up in the cabin with Elden for weeks on end, and frowned. He hoped to be able to take the pair to Fort Laramie as soon as possible.

"Say, look at that peak south of here!" Elden declared. "It must be the highest on the continent! Maybe you should name it after yourself so one day you'll have your name on the map."

"That particular mountain already has a name," Nate said. "Long's Peak."

"Has somebody climbed it, then?"

"No. Back in '19 and '20, a man by the name of Stephen Long, a major in the Army, explored this part of the country for the government."

"I remember!" Elden said. "The Yellowstone Expedition."

"Yes. Long happened to see the peak and mistook it for Pike's Peak. Seems his sense of geography was a little flawed. Some of the old-time trappers, in fact, claimed that he couldn't find his hind end with written directions. So the trappers hereabouts took to calling the peak after him."

"What about the rest of these mountains? Do they have names too?"

"Some are known by Indian words."

"But none have been named after white men?"

"Not yet."

"How marvelous!" Elden crowed. "Why, I could have one named after me, couldn't I? I could just pick one out that strikes my fancy and call it Leonard Mountain."

"If you want," Nate said, concealing his amusement at the childish notion. "But getting some mapmaker to print a map with your name on it might take some doing."

"It's worth the try. Just think of it! A legacy to leave future generations." Elden chuckled. "Don't you want people to remember you after you die?"

"I've no hankering to be famous, if that's what you mean. My family and friends will remember me. Those who don't know me hardly matter."

"All men matter. We're all brothers spiritually, after all."

Nate glanced back. "You never impressed me as being the religious type," he commented.

"What an unkind thing to say. I may not wear a halo, but I went to church when I was younger. I've read a goodly portion of the Bible." Elden adopted a hurt tone. "I'm not totally ignorant, despite what you suppose."

The trail hooked around a cluster of pines and the lake unfolded before them. Nate walked to the edge and studied the layer of ice that had formed along the shore, judging it to be an inch or so thick and extending a dozen feet out into the water. Kneeling, he set down the bucket, then pounded the ice once with his fist. The surface developed a hairline crack but stayed intact otherwise. He scoured his immediate vicinity for the hole Winona must have made when last she drew water, but there was no evidence of one. Ice had closed over it.

"Are there fish in this lake?" Elden inquired.

"Quite a few."

"How about if we go ice fishing later? I haven't done that since I was a little boy. It would be great fun."

"If we have the time," Nate said, with as much enthusiasm as he might evince for wrestling a grizzly. Rising, he moved into the trees, seeking a suitable limb. With everything buried by snow, he had to search for over five minutes before finding the stout branch he needed. Wiping it off, he returned to the lake, where Elden was pacing back and forth to keep warm.

"Wouldn't it have been smarter to build the cabin closer to the lake so a body wouldn't have as far to go on winter days?" the greenhorn asked.

"If my uncle had built it too close, the deer and elk would all go to the other end to drink. This way, if we need meat and we spot an animal close enough, we can shoot right out the door or the window."

A swishing sound drew Nate's attention upward to a solitary sleek raven in slow flight to the west. Every beat of its big black wings was clearly audible in the quiet of the woodland. He watched it sail over his home, then knelt once again and gouged the tapered end of the branch into the ice. Working methodically, he gradually chipped away until he had a hole larger than the bucket.

Behind him Elden paced and paced.

Nate dipped the bucket in, being careful not to get his hands wet since the water was so cold his fingers would freeze in seconds. Once the bucket was filled to the brim, he carefully lifted it out of the hole and started to stand.

"Here. I'll hold that for you," Elden offered, and leaned down to grip the handle. Suddenly his left foot slipped. His leg shot out from under him and he stumbled forward, his arms flailing the air as he desperately attempted to retain his balance.

Halfway upright, Nate saw Elden sliding toward him and tried to step aside. But the next instant Elden slammed into his shoulder and sent him flying—straight into the lake.

Chapter Eight

As Nate King plunged toward the ice, he instinctively let go of the bucket, took a breath, and held the air in his lungs. In a twinkling the ice rushed up to meet him and he heard a tremendous crackling noise. Frantically he clutched for a handhold, but all his fingers found were slick, loose chunks which offered no purchase. Then frigid wetness enveloped him and started to drag him toward the bottom of the lake.

Panic clawed at Nate's mind. He had to fight the terror, fight to stay calm and do what had to be done. As he sank, he twisted, shrugging out of his heavy buffalo robe. His buckskins were already soaked, his skin prickling as if from a thousand cold, barbed needles. Looking up, he saw large and small pieces of ice foating where he had broken through, and close to the shore Elden's distorted moon face gawking down at him.

With a powerful flick of his legs, Nate shot to the surface, coming up alongside an unbroken section. "Help me!" he roared, thrusting an arm out at Leonard.

Elden stood only three feet away. He could have reached out and grasped Nate's fingers. But he didn't. Instead, he glanced fearfully down at the water, spun, and raced off up the trail, shouting, "Hang on! I'll fetch help!"

For a fleeting moment sheer rage dominated Nate's being. Then he started to sink again and he had to concentrate on staying alive. He lunged, flinging himself partway out onto the ice, heard another rending crash, and went belly-first into the freezing water. His feet lashed every which way, searching for a foothold he could use to propel himself onto the shore. At this spot, however, there was a sheer drop-off, and he only treaded water. And not for long at that.

Lethargy was setting in. Nate could feel his movements becoming more and more sluggish. He knew the bone-numbing temperature was slowing the blood in his veins. Unless he escaped from the lake and swiftly, he would succumb to the cold and drown.

Once again Nate stroked to the surface. It took longer this time, and his lungs were close to bursting. Greedily he sucked in air and became aware of water turning solid on his face, covering his mouth and nose. He swiped at the forming ice, clearing his nasal passages so he could breathe again, yet in doing so he neglected to pump his legs and sank a third time.

The world was a blur. The underwater realm was shrouded in gloom. Nate blinked, or tried to, but his eyelids appeared locked wide open. An air bubble rose upward from the tip of his nose as he dropped lower and lower. Above him beckoned the opening in the ice. If only he could reach it!

Nate thought of Winona, Zach, and Evelyn, of his

love for them and theirs for him, and suddenly he simply refused to die. He wanted to live, to see them again, to hold them in his arms and know the joy of being a husband and a father. Gritting his teeth in savage determination, he pumped his arms and legs, forcing his limbs to cooperate despite the death grip of the icy water. At a snail's pace, he rose. His chest hurt, his lungs were screaming for relief. He felt water in his ears, water in his nose, and then, to his dismay, water in his mouth.

Abruptly, light flooded his eyes. Nate bobbed to the surface and gulped in ragged breaths. He was near another intact strip of ice. With no other recourse available, he managed to prop his forearms on top of the strip and wiggle a few inches out of the water. Amazingly, the ice held. He could breath without difficulty, but he dreaded being pitched back into the depths if he moved too strenuously and literally shattered his only hope of salvation.

Nate rested a few seconds, conserving his strength for what came next. He glanced toward the cabin but saw only trees. Faintly, he believed he heard shouting. Winona was coming to the rescue. The question was: Would she get there in time?

Swallowing nervously, Nate edged higher onto the strip, squirming like a snake or a worm, applying as little pressure as he could. He heard a soft snap, paused to be sure the whole sheet wasn't crumbling, then crawled out further. There was no longer any sensation in his legs, so he couldn't tell if they were still in the water or not, although he thought they were. The shore was only two feet away. Only two feet, yet it might as well be miles.

Nate stretched out his right arm and his fingers brushed the bank. He probed in the snow for something, anything, to hold onto. All he found was yielding snow. His anxiety mounting, afraid he would freeze before attaining safety, he extended his left arm. Still a secure purchase eluded him.

Then the ice began to splinter. Nate heard the crackling and saw cobwebs lance outward from under his body. In seconds the strip would give way as the others had. He cried out, or tried to, and summoned the last of his reserve of stamina so he could hurl himself at solid ground. The lower half of his body angled downward, sinking into the lake. He was on the brink of going under for the final time when he executed a rolling flip, and to his astonishment rolled right out onto the bank.

Profound relief rooted Nate there. He shook and shivered, his teeth chattering wildly, and tried to resist the fatigue and debilitating chill that threatened to make him lose consciousness. To his dismay, he suddenly felt his body sliding slowly down into the water. He had to move or all his effort would have been for naught.

Nate got his left hand on the ground and dug his fingers in, trying to arrest his descent. His right arm contacted the water. He recoiled, jerking away, and in doing so increased the speed of his slide. His life hung suspended on the scales of Fate, and in another moment he would be underwater once more.

"Nooooo!"

The piercing cry heralded the arrival of Nate's rescuers. Strong hands grasped him and hauled him onto level ground. Nate saw Winona's face, and Zach's, and he longed to hug them close but he was too frozen to move.

"Husband! Husband!" Winona said in Shoshone. "Can you talk?" Her fingers pried at the ice covering his face and neck, and she cut herself in her haste.

"Pa!" Zach added in despair.

Try as Nate might, he couldn't get his mouth to work. His lips moved only a fraction, his tongue only twitched.

"We must get him inside quickly," Winona announced in English, addressing someone out of Nate's line of vision. "Don't stand there! Help!"

Selena and Elden Leonard appeared, their heads hanging above Nate's like disembodied apparitions. Had Nate been able to speak, he would have cursed Elden mercilessly. As it was, he had to let himself be lifted and carted off toward the cabin. Twice Elden slipped on the way there, and the second time the back of Nate's head hit the earth with jarring force.

"Be careful, darn you!" Zach shouted.

Even though Nate could barely move and had little idea of what was going on around him, he knew by the sudden warmth when they entered the cabin. He was carried over close to the flames and set down gently on his back on the bearskin rug. The heat felt so deliciously wonderful he had an urge to crawl into the fire.

"Blankets, Zach," Winona was saying. "Selena, we need to boil water. Will Elden and you run back down to the lake and retrieve the bucket? I saw it near the broken ice."

"On our way," Selena said.

Moist palms touched Nate's cheeks as his wife lowered her face close to his. Tears rimmed her eyes. "Rest easy, loved one. I will have you thawed out soon."

The gratitude Nate yearned to express had to wait until his voice returned. He tried to speak, but all that came out was a strangled gurgle. Weariness pervading every part of his being, he closed his eyes and savored merely being alive. Fingers plucked at his drenched buckskins and they were stripped from his still-shivering frame. Something soft touched his skin, rubbing him dry, and he cracked his lids to see his son using a towel. The boy looked so thoroughly worried that Nate mustered a wan grin to show he was feeling better already. Then drowsiness set in, and his last sensation before drifting off to sleep was that of blankets being draped over him.

A crackling sound brought Nate around with a start and he sat bolt upright. It reminded him of the cracking of the ice, and for a few seconds he imagined he was struggling once again to escape the icy grasp of the deceptively serene lake. His arms swung wildly and he cried out.

"You are safe, husband. Be calm."

Nate saw Winona at his side and felt her hands restraining his wrists. Suddenly weak, he sagged against her and kissed her on the neck. "I thought . . ." he croaked, and left the statement unfinished.

"We brought you inside, remember?" Winona said. "You've been asleep for a long time. It must be after midnight."

"Midnight?" Nate repeated in astonishment as he gazed around the cabin. Zach was curled up on blankets in the corner with Blaze, their usual resting place. Several times Nate had offered to build the boy a bed, but Zach had always declined, claiming he wouldn't be able to sleep without the comfort of a hard surface to lie on.

The Leonards were in the same corner as the saddle, side by side under a heavy quilt, Selena in peaceful repose, Elden doing a superb imitation of a angry grizzly every time he snored.

Winona noticed where he was gazing and commented, "You were fortunate, my dearest, that Elden reached us quickly. Had he not been with you, there would have been no one to come for help and you might have frozen to death."

"Had he not been with me, I wouldn't have fallen in," Nate informed her. At length he explained exactly what had occurred, concluding with, "The man is a walking menace. I can hardly wait to get him to Fort Laramie."

"Why are you so bitter toward him? It was an accident, was it not?" Winona said.

"So? You know as well as I do that a person has to be more careful in the wilderness. Any accident, no matter how small, can be downright deadly."

"Still, there is no reason to be mad at him. It is not his fault he is so helpless. Selena told me their parents raised him as the pet of the family. Poor Elden never did or learned much of anything as a boy, and his manhood reflects this."

Mildly annoyed that Winona would defend the greenhorn, Nate said nothing. He had no inclination to get into a squabble over the subject. All that mattered to him at the moment was recovering as quickly as possible. His cheek rested on her chest, his arms lay around her waist. Once again his eyelids drooped and he sank into sleep.

When next Nate awakened, sunlight was streaming in the window and somewhere outside sparrows were chirping. He was flat on his back, covered by a soft three-point Hudson's Bay blanket Winona had traded for at the last Rendezvous. Folded on the floor close by were his dry buckskins and moccasins, along with his two pistols, butcher knife, and tomahawk. No one else was in the cabin.

Feeling invigorated after his long rest, Nate hurriedly dressed, his eyes on the door in case it should open. He didn't want the greenhorns, particularly Selena, walking in on him before he was done. He checked the flint-locks and discovered Winona had emptied out the wet powder, cleaned both weapons, and reloaded them. The knife he inspected minutely for dry specks of water, but there were none. With her usual efficiency, Winona had applied a drop of the oil to each side and wiped the long blade clean. The oil helped to prevent rust from forming, which was the bane of all frontiersmen and the reason Nate hadn't used the knife to chop a hole in the ice. The tomahawk, another possession they had picked up at a Rendezvous, had a metal head, and he checked this too before slipping the handle underneath his leather belt. Neither his clothes nor his weapons were any the worse for having been submerged.

Dressed and armed, Nate strode to the counter to drink from the bucket. He was puzzled to find fresh strips of jerked venison lying nearby, one of which he nibbled on as he stepped to the door and threw it open. Brilliant sunshine made him squint, and he shielded his eyes with a hand as he walked out.

From the south came voices mingled with laughter. Nate went through the trees until he saw a low hill, one of his favorite spots to go when he wanted to be alone with his thoughts. Careening down the snowy slope on a wide, curved piece of bark was his son, cackling crazily all the while. The makeshift sled came to a rest just yards away.

"Pa! You're on your feet again! How do you feel?" Zach asked, springing up and giving Nate a hug.

"Fine. Really fine."

There was a call from the top of the hill, and Nate waved at his wife. The Leonards, all smiles, were with her. "What do you have here?" he inquired of his son.

"Elden gave me the notion," Zach answered. "He was telling me about the sledding he used to do in New York and I got to thinking about a way to do the same. Took me a long time to carve off a piece strong enough to take my weight."

"Well, I guess Elden is good for something after all."

Zach blinked. "Why do you talk like that, Pa? Elden is all right once you get to know him." Picking up the sled in both hands, he headed back up the slope.

"So everyone seems to think," Nate said to himself. Just the day before, he wryly reflected, his son had disliked Elden immensely; now the two were apparently fast friends. This revelation, coming as it did on the heels of Winona's defense of Elden the previous night, bothered Nate, although he told himself it shouldn't. Just because he disliked Elden, there was no reason his family had to do the same.

About to join in the frolic, Nate saw Winona descending and waited for her. She scrutinized him from head to toe as a mother hen might an ailing chick.

"You seem fully recovered, but how do you feel?"

"Hungry enough to eat a steak raw," Nate admitted, adding as he displayed the half-eaten strip of jerky. "Where did this come from? I thought we were out of food."

"Zach shot a doe while you were gone. He wants to be the one to tell you all about it, so be sure to ask him later." Winona touched a palm to his brow. "The fever you had is gone. If I get a full meal in you, you should be your old self again."

"That's not all I need," Nate told her with a mischievous twinkle in his eyes.

"Behave, husband. We have visitors."

"Don't remind me."

"Are you still upset over the accident? It is not like you to hold a mistake against someone." Winona smiled at the Leonards. "And they have both been very courteous and helpful. Selena helped me prepare breakfast, and Elden helped Zach gather grass and cottonwood bark for the horses."

Not in the least eager to discuss the Leonards, Nate moved around behind his wife and parted the coverings on the cradleboard so he could see his daughter. Evelyn smiled and worked her lips, her hands waving excitedly. "Hello, precious," he said, bending to give her a kiss on the tip of her nose.

"Whheeeeeeeee!"

Turning, Nate watched his son slide down the hill once more. "How big was this doe you mentioned?" he inquired over his shoulder.

"Not very big at all. With two extra mouths to feed, the meat we have left will last no more than seven or eight sleeps. Longer if we only eat only one meal a day."

The information vexed Nate. He dared not leave his family without enough provisions when he escorted the Leonards to Fort Laramie, which meant he had to go off hunting again before he could get the pair out of his hair. But he didn't much like the idea of leaving his wife and children alone with the Easterners, although he couldn't quite say why he felt uneasy about the prospect. Perhaps because of Elden. The only other alternative, though, was to take Elden with him when he went after game, a ridiculous plan in light of Leonard's inexperience; the man would not only slow him down, but probably scare off anything worth shooting.

As if Winona could read his thoughts, she said, "You should not have to go far this time. Where there is one deer there are usually more. Find those the doe was bedding down with and we will have enough meat to last us until spring."

"I can try," Nate said doubtfully, remembering the many days he had scoured their valley from end to end without finding so much as a single set of fresh tracks. The doe might have been part of a herd passing through on its way elsewhere, a herd long gone, in which case he'd have to hunt far afield again. And he had only himself to blame. Next year, he vowed, he would stock up in the fall with enough jerky and pemmican to last a decade.

"All will be well, husband," Winona said, reading his feelings in his face. "It is most unlike you to be so bothered over events over which you have no control."

"I'm fine," Nate said, even though deep down he wasn't, even though deep down a persistent but vague sense that something was wrong continued to bother him. He'd never felt anything like it, which compounded his confusion.

What on earth could it be?

On the crown of the hill Elden Leonard gave his sister a nudge and snickered. "Look at them down there! Like cattle being led to the slaughter, they don't have the foggiest idea what they're in for."

"Not so loud, idiot," Selena said.

Elden saw Zach go over to talk to Nate and Winona. "They can't hear us all the way up here." He rubbed his hands together and blew on his fingers. "Besides, I'm not scared of an ignorant trapper, a squaw, and a half-breed kid. As for the baby—I can hardly wait."

"King isn't to be taken lightly. I've learned a great deal about him from his wife," Selena disclosed. "Did you know he's slain more grizzly bears than any other white man or Indian alive? He's killed so many, the Indians call him Grizzly Killer."

"A trusting buffoon by any other name is still a buffoon."

"Do you have any brains at all? I tell you that King is as dangerous as those savages who caught us, and

Winona and Zach can give us grief too if we're not extremely cautious."

"The bitch and the brat? Oh, come now."

Selena spun, her back to the family below so none of them would see her expression. "Damn you, Elden!" she hissed. "I won't have you spoiling this like you've spoiled so much else for us. You will keep a rein on that tongue of yours and do nothing to arouse their suspicions."

"I'll be a paragon of circumspection."

"If your intelligence was the equal of your vocabulary," Selena said in disgust, "we wouldn't be here right now. We'd be living in luxury in New York City." She jabbed a finger into his chest. "You're to blame for this disaster, not me. But as usual, I'm the one who had to save us."

Elden smirked. "And a fine job you did too. Were those Bloods part of your plan?"

For a moment Selena appeared on the verge of slapping him; her hand shot up, rigid as a board, and her face bloomed scarlet with rage. Then she stiffened and glanced around to see if Nate or Winona had noticed. On verifying they hadn't, she lowered her arm and spoke in a clipped, precise manner, every word stinging her brother as would the flick of a whip. "You have always been a complete and utter ass, brother of mine, and you always will be. Where would you be without me? I'll tell you. You would be rotting away in a dank cell in prison, provided, of course, you were still alive." Her eyes were slits, her voice gravelly. "If you will refresh your memory, it was I who saved you this time by slipping that dagger between Bascomb's ribs."

"How was I to know he would follow me after I picked up the satchel?"

"Dunderhead! You should never take anything for

granted. Haven't you learned that by now?"

Elden scowled and jammed his hands into his pockets. He kicked at the snow, nearly fell, then cursed. "I hate these mountains," he muttered after he had calmed sufficiently. "I hate trees and rocks. I hate snow. I hate bushes and wild animals. I hate Nate King and his whore squaw. I hate—"

"Enough," Selena said. "Don't fall apart on me now." Her red lips curved upward as she affectionately stroked his chin. "I need you at your best, darling. Everything must be done exactly as I tell you."

"I tried at the lake. He never suspected I bumped into him on purpose." Elden spat. "It wasn't my fault he survived."

"You did just fine. I don't blame you."

"What next, then?" Elden asked. "I say we wait until they're asleep tonight and slit their throats."

"And if one of them should wake up and give a yell before we're done?" Selena shook her head. "Why take needless risks? No, we will exercise patience, my brother. We will wait for an opportunity to arise, and then we will dispose of either King or his wife and make it appear to be an accident. Once one of them is out of the way, the other one will be easier to kill. And with the parents gone, the children will pose no problem at all."

"It doesn't make a difference which one we do first?"

"None whatsoever."

"Good." Elden's fleshy face acquired a flinty cast. "I just hope it's King himself. No one treats me the way he did. He'll learn the hard way I'm not the weakling he thinks."

"Just don't faint again."

"You saw that wolf! You can't blame me."

A titter was Selena's response. "At least you pulled the wool over King's eyes. He would never guess that you've killed about a dozen people."

"Eleven, to be precise." Elden stared at the trapper and sneered, "The mighty Grizzly Killer will make it an even dozen."

Chapter Nine

Elden Leonard was dreaming. He was imagining himself dressed in the finest clothes, with an expensive beaver hat crowning his head, a flowing cape over his shoulders, and a polished cane in his right hand. With deft skill he twirled the gold-handled cane and beamed at the vision of loveliness whose arm was linked in his. Selena smiled and winked, the tilt of her eyebrow hinting at the pleasures to come later that evening. The next moment, however, the ground under them began to heave and toss. His first thought was that New York City was being struck by an earthquake. Then he roused sufficiently to realize he was quaking because of a firm hand on his shoulder, and he heard his name whispered over and over. With an effort he opened his eyes and saw Nate King standing over him. "What?" he asked, befuddled by sleep. "What is it?"

"Keep your voice down," Nate said. "We don't want

to wake the others."

Elden blinked and gazed around in confusion. The interior of the cabin was dimly lit by a few embers sputtering in the fireplace. He had the impression night reigned outside, so he said, "What's the matter? What time is it?"

"Get up," Nate ordered.

"Why?" Elden responded. The lingering images of his dream beckoned, and he longed to return to his fantasy rather than confront depressing reality.

"We're going hunting."

"You must be jesting," Elden said. "I don't know the first thing about tracking and shooting animals."

"It's time you learned. Get up."

Irritated by the mountain man's insistence, Elden rose on his elbows and declared, "I've never shot so much as a pheasant, I tell you. What good would I be out there? Go hunting yourself and let me enjoy my sleep." He began to lower himself down when steely hands seized him by the front of his shirt and he was literally yanked out from under his comfortable blankets.

"You're coming with me whether you like the notion or not," Nate growled. "So get your shoes on and meet me outside. I have the horses saddled and our supplies packed." Pivoting, he stalked out, quietly closing the door behind him.

"Of all the nerve!" Elden said under his breath. Anger sparked by the rude treatment he had received had rendered him fully awake, and he experienced a near irresistible urge to smash something. He glanced down at Selena, who had slept undisturbed through the humiliating episode, and had half a mind to give her a kick to wake her up so he could inform her of King's behavior. But he controlled himself and did as the trapper had commanded. Their plan called for them to cooperate with the Kings in every way, to do everything in their power to convince the frontier couple that they were as innocent and friendly as newborn babes. Treachery, after all, was more effectively executed if the victims were totally unsuspecting.

A biting cold gust of wind bit into Elden as he stepped outside. Pulling his coat tighter around him, he gazed at the twinkling stars and groused, "It's not even daylight yet."

"But it will be in a short while," Nate responded, jabbing his rifle at the eastern sky where faint pink smudges adorned the horizon. "Mount up and we'll be on our way."

"But why so early?" Elden couldn't help asking as he awkwardly climbed onto the mare King had waiting for him. "It's so dark we couldn't see to shoot a thing."

"Deer and elk are most active two times during the day," Nate patiently explained. "At dawn and at sunset. The rest of the time they're holed up in the brush." Turning his horse, he rode toward the lake.

Elden, inwardly seething, reluctantly trailed the trapper. The only thing worse than being forced out of a warm bed at such an ungodly hour, in his estimation, was being made to bounce around on another horse. He never had liked horses much; never had been fond of riding. His posterior and his thighs always hurt abominably after a few hours in the saddle. He was absolutely convinced that his behind was simply too delicate to endure such abuse, and he intended to never, ever sit astride one of the smelly animals again once he and his sister were settled in the Oregon Territory.

A tree limb snatched at Elden's arm and he wrenched it loose. As if he didn't have enough to worry about! he fumed. And suddenly inspiration flared. A crafty glint came into his eyes. Rather than be upset, he recognized he should be grateful to King for this golden opportunity.

Elden snickered softly. Here might be the chance he was looking for to dispose of the mountain man! In such rugged terrain accidents were bound to happen. All he had to do was stay alert, and when the right moment came, do whatever was needed. A cliff would be the ideal place, since he'd only have to give King a push and his problems would be solved. "Say," he said as casually as he could, "why are we staying here where it's so flat? Shouldn't we be up higher among the peaks?"

There was a mild hint of surprise at the suggestion in Nate's tone when he answered, "No, we shouldn't. The snow is even deeper up there, and the deer and elk can't find enough to eat. So they wander down into the valleys to forage until spring."

"Stupid creatures," Elden whispered to himself in disappointment that his cliff scheme had been dashed. He scanned the countryside, considering a number of devious alternatives. Foremost was pushing King into the lake again if they strayed close enough, and this time he would stay there and use a limb to keep King underwater until the deed was done. If they didn't go near the lake, he might wait until King was distracted and bash the man's brains in with a heavy rock. Later he could tell Winona her husband had fallen from the stallion when the stallion was scared by a snake. He liked that idea immensely until he recalled reading somewhere that snakes weren't active in cold weather. So he'd blame it on a lizard, he mused with a shrug. It made small difference.

Nate swung to the south of the lake, through woodland bordering thick brush which in turn bordered the water. The sky brightened rapidly and a rosy glow suffused the line of mountains to the east. Presently he came on a small clearing where he reined up, then put a finger to his lips to enjoin silence.

Elden nodded and slid down. His legs were stiff, his joints sore. He tied the mare to a branch, saw King gesture, and walked over.

"From here on you can't make any noise," Nate whispered. "Remember that deer can hear a man cough from a quarter of a mile off."

"You exaggerate surely."

"Not by much." Nate moved around the stallion. "Before we get started, I have something for you."

"What is it?" Elden asked suspiciously, suspecting King would demand that he tote a heavy pack into the undergrowth so King's hands would be free for firing. Disgusted, he hugged himself and stamped his feet to warm up his legs.

"I told you not to make any noise."

"Oh. Sorry." Elden scowled and stared into the distance. He thought of his sister, snug and warm back in the cabin, and wished he could change places with her. The way things were going, it would be a miracle if he got to kill King. This hunt, he fumed, was a waste of his time.

"Here. You'll need this."

Elden turned and gawked in welcome surprise. He wanted to whoop with delight, but satisfied himself by smiling gratefully. "Why, thank you," he said.

Nate King was handing him a rifle.

At that instant, back in the cabin, Selena Leonard opened her eyes and stretched languidly. Her left arm, which should have brushed her brother, fanned only air, and she shifted to see if he had rolled off in his sleep. On finding him gone, she sat up mystified. A quick look showed Nate King was also missing, leading her to the conclusion the pair had gone somewhere.

Running a hand through her hair, Selena studied the sleeping forms of Winona, Zach, and the infant. How easy it would be, she thought, to slit their throats as Elden had suggested. Strongly tempted, she rose to a knee and glanced at a drawer under the counter where she knew Winona kept several knives. If she did the deeds swiftly, all three would die without crying out. Then she'd hide behind the door, wait for Nate King to return, and plunge the blade into his back as he entered.

Selena slowly rose and took a step. Movement near Zach stopped her. Her breath caught in her throat when she saw the wolf lift its shaggy head and regard her coldly. In her eagerness she had forgotten all about it. The beast's face was clouded in shadow, lending it a menacing aspect. Selena glanced again at the drawer, then changed her mind. Given the wolf's attachment to the boy and the family, it might well attack her at the slightest threatening gesture, and she entertained no illusions about how she'd fare in a struggle with the powerful animal.

"Good morning."

The gentle greeting almost made Selena jump. She faced Winona, who was rising, and replied, "Oh, dear. I hope I didn't wake you."

Winona nodded at the window where a telltale feeble blush of light served as a harbinger of the oncoming dawn. "I always awaken at this time, without fail." She picked up the baby and moved to the counter. "Breakfast will be ready shortly. There is still plenty of water in the bucket so you may wash up if you would like."

"I'm fine," Selena lied, because in truth she felt grimier than she had ever felt in her life. She couldn't recall the last time she had enjoyed a hot bath or washed her hair.

And her clothes were equally grimy. "Do you happen to know where my brother got to?" she inquired.

"My husband said something last night about possibly going hunting at dawn," Winona answered. "He might have taken your brother along."

"Elden will love that. He just adores the outdoors."

"What would you care to do today?" Winona asked.

"My only interest is in helping you to repay you for your hospitality," Selena answered sweetly. "Sewing, cooking, whatever. You just name it."

"I plan to check my snares today. You may come along if you like."

"Snares?"

Winona bobbed her chin as she took pemmican from a cupboard. "Among my people, the Shoshones, the men do most of the hunting. But the women are expected to add to the cooking pot also. In season we gather plants and wild fruit and roots. And while we do not go after buffalo or antelope, we do add our share of meat by catching small animals in snares." She paused. "My mother taught me the skill, and she learned from her mother before her. Generation to generation, the knowledge is handed down."

"How fascinating," Selena said, somehow managing to keep the sarcasm out of her voice.

"I learned how to find the game trails and rabbit runs the animals use regularly, how to pick the best spots for catching them, and how to make different kinds of snares as the occasion requires."

Selena moved closer and smiled at the baby. "What amazes me most about you is how well you've learned English. I know I've mentioned it once before, but you speak it perfectly."

"Nate and Shakespeare say I have a natural gift."

"Shakespeare?"

"McNair. Nate's closest friend, a man who has lived in these mountains longer than any other white. He lives north of us a ways. Any day now he might stop by for a visit and you can meet him in person."

"Oh?" Selena said, her jaw muscles twitching at the distressing news. "Are you expecting him?"

"No. He just swings on by whenever he wants. If we are lucky, he'll bring his wife along. Blue Water Woman is a wonderful person."

"I hope he does," Selena lied. She could just see the couple showing up after she and Elden had killed the Kings but before they were able to dispose of the bodies! Then there would be two more to kill, and that much more work to do lugging the corpses away.

A few minutes later Zach woke up and went out to gather wood for the fire.

The wolf, Selena noticed, had not budged. She looked at it several times, and each time it was looking right back at her. As an experiment, she moved to the fireplace. The wolf's eyes never left her. Acting on the assumption she might be able to make friends with it, she started to walk over. A chilling, barely audible growl halted her in the middle of a stride.

"Was that Blaze?" Winona asked, turning.

"Sure was," Selena said. "I was about to pet him, but I guess he doesn't like me."

"We can't have that," Winona said. Opening the door, she gestured and yelled, "Out you go, Blaze! Come on!"

The wolf twitched an ear, nothing more.

"You heard me," Winona persisted. She slapped a thigh and pointed at the snow. "If you can not be nice to our guests, you are not allowed to stay. Now go!"

A ripple of fear made Selena's pulse race when the wolf suddenly stood and took a step toward her. She

thought it was about to spring. A yell from Winona
elicited another low growl. But head low, Blaze padded
across the floor and into the sunlight of a new day.

"I am very sorry," Winona said as she closed the door.
"I have no idea what caused him to behave the way he
did. Wolves can be so unpredictable."

"Do you think it's safe to keep around?" Selena asked.

"Blaze would never hurt any of us. However, if you
would feel safer, I'll keep him outside until Nate takes
you down to Fort Laramie. We want you to feel comfortable during your stay here."

"Oh, I do. I like this cabin so much I wouldn't mind
owning it myself."

"Nate's uncle built this," Winona said, giving the wall
a pat. "He would never part with it."

Taking a seat at the table, Selena pondered her next
move while waiting for her breakfast. Events had worked
out in her favor; temporarily she was alone with the
squaw and the child. All she had to do was get her
hands on a weapon. Since Winona was at the counter, she'd need to use something other than a knife. But
what? she asked herself.

Selena saw a pair of rifles leaning against the wall
near the door. Either would suffice, but she didn't know
if they were loaded. And using a gun would make a lot
of noise, maybe alerting the boy. Prudence dictated she
do the job quietly. As her gaze roved along the walls, she
spied an Indian lance in the same corner as the bed.

Standing without making any noise, Selena moved
slowly. Winona was facing the counter, engrossed in
preparing coffee. All Selena had to do was scoop up
the lance and bury it in the Shoshone's back before
Winona turned around. She tiptoed to within a yard of
the weapon.

Selena reached for the lance. Her fingertips brushed

the smooth shaft, and she was on the verge of grasping the weapon when she heard the door open and a gust of air fanned her hair. Spinning, she forced a carefree grin and held her hands at her waist in an attitude of perfect innocence as Zach King strode in bearing an armful of chopped wood, which he carried to the fireplace and set down.

"Want me to fetch more, Ma?"

"That should be enough for a while," Winona told him.

The boy closed the door, then fed some of the logs to the fire and squatted with his hands extended to warm them. "It's cold out there, but not quite as bad as yesterday," he commented.

Concealing the bitter disappointment she felt, Selena moved to the table and took a seat. Now she must wait until Winona and the breed were separated again. The boy was young, but he must be viewed as potentially dangerous; he always had his rifle with him, and in addition had a big knife and a tomahawk wedged under his belt. She entertained no doubts that he knew how to use all three weapons proficiently. Frontier brats, she had discovered, learned at an early age the skills they needed to survive in the wild.

The meager fare Winona was able to offer for breakfast did little to elevate Selena's spirits. She munched half-heartedly on the pemmican, sipped the weak coffee, and daydreamed of the many breakfasts she had enjoyed in New York; thick, juicy strips of bacon, a plate heaped with eggs, hot toast or muffins, and all the hot chocolate she could drink had been her ideal way to start a new day.

After the meal Winona busied herself at the counter for a short while. Selena cradled the baby in her arms and pretended she liked infants by talking gibberish and tickling Evelyn under the chin. She speculated on how her brother was faring, and hoped Elden would find a means of dispatching Nate King. The more she thought about the idea of using the cabin as a hideaway until springtime, the more she liked it. Their only problem would be finding enough food until the weather warmed. They'd simply have to shoot anything and everything they saw moving.

"Ready to go check those snares?" Winona inquired.

Selena brightened. Here was the answer to her problem, and she hadn't even realized it! If she could learn how to set snares, then she could provide a steady supply of meat. Elden and she would have no difficulty hanging on. "Yes," she answered cheerfully. "I'm looking forward to it."

Winona donned a buffalo robe, belted a knife around her waist, and selected a rifle from those near the door. "We will be back as soon as we can," she informed her son. "Please watch your sister carefully. She's sleeping now, and she should nap for a long time if you are quiet."

Zach glanced up. "What if she wakes up, though, and wants to be fed? She can kick up a fuss when she's of a mind."

"Try rocking her in your arms. If that does not work, go outside and yell for us. I won't be far off."

Selena's interest perked up. "The snares are close to the cabin?" she asked.

"Most of them are," Winona said.

Important news, Selena reflected. She must make certain she disposed of the Shoshone quietly. And she must remember to keep an eye out for Nate King. Bundling into her coat, she trailed Winona to the doorway. "I don't mean to bother you," she said tentatively.

"What is it?" Winona inquired, her hand on the latch.

"After all that's happened to me, I'm a bit frightened about going back out into the woods," Selena said with a convincing tremor. "Do you suppose I could impose on your kindness and ask for a weapon?"

"Of course," Winona said, and went to grab another flintlock.

"I'm not a very good shot," Selena said quickly. "I'd probably be better off with a knife or one of those tomohawkens or whatever they're called, if you must know the truth."

"Oh." Winona glanced around, then walked to a drawer, opened it, and sorted through a number of tools and other items. "We do not have any tomahawks to spare, but there is a . . ." She grinned and pulled out a knife in a beaded scabbard. "This belonged to my mother. I keep it stored away because I don't want to lose or damage it, but for you I will make an exception."

"Why, that's very gracious of you," Selena said, taking the knife.

"For a friend I can do no less."

The knife went into Selena's right pocket as she walked from the cabin. Just as Winona closed the door behind them, a shot cracked in the distance, to the east, from near the vicinity of the lake.

"Perhaps Nate or Elden has found us meat," Winona said hopefully.

"I hope for my brother's sake that he has made himself useful by shooting *something*," Selena mentioned, adding, "If he got what he went after, he'll be so proud of himself."

The sun was suspended above the eastern mountains, and the air, as Zach had indicated, was frigid but not bitterly so. Glistening and sparkling in the bright sunlight, the snow lent the deep forest a chaste, untrammeled aspect. The Rockies themselves radiated a sublime beauty befitting their majesty.

Selena Leonard never noticed. All she cared about was killing Winona King. She fingered the hilt of the knife in her pocket, biding her time until an opportunity should arise. And as she fondled it, she talked up a storm, asking every question she could think of related to the technique of setting snares so she would know enough to keep Elden and her alive once the Kings were dead.

Winona was pleased to find her guest so interested and went on at length, explaining how to find the narrow pathways in the undergrowth that served as connecting links between watering areas, bedding spots, and feeding grounds for a variety of animals. She elaborated on how the width and depth of the runs showed the type of animals using them.

Selena was an attentive learner. As the two of them trekked from snare to snare, she acquired an understanding of the different kinds, and how to judge the sort to be employed from the type of animal traveling the run and the lay of the terrain itself. Peg snares, rock snares, hook snares, she became familiar with them all, and more. So engrossed did she become, in fact, that she was shocked when Winona made the following remark:

"Well, we only have two more snares to check, and they are both up this gorge. Then we can head home."

Halting in surprise, Selena watched the Indian woman advance into a wide gap between towering rock walls. She looked to the right and the left, insuring Nate King was nowhere in sight. Then, drawing the knife that had belonged to Winona's mother, she hurried forward to deal the fatal blow.

Chapter Ten

Earlier, at the very moment the two women had ventured from the cabin, Elden Leonard had been following Nate along the south shore of the lake. He'd been profoundly miserable, on the verge of tears. Not only was his stomach empty and constantly growling to remind him of his hunger, but the cold had sapped his strength and energy to the point he felt unable to go another hundred yards. Several times in the span of a minute he glared at the broad back in front of him and fingered the trigger of his flintlock, yet each time he removed the finger and pressed on.

Elden was scared to do the deed. He feared he might miss, or his shot would spare a vital organ, thereby giving King time to turn and shoot at him. And as much as Elden wanted Nate King dead, as much as Elden couldn't wait to spit on the trapper's lifeless face, most of all Elden wanted to go on living. He had mentally vowed not to commit himself until success was certain.

The morning had consisted of alternate periods of hiding in the brush and hiking to different vantage points. Elden had soon grown tired of the boring routine. Twice he had suggested to King they were wasting their time, but the man had ignored him. And Elden sorely hated being ignored. His sister did it far too frequently; his parents had been little better. Being ignored made him feel useless, insignificant, as he had often felt as a child, a feeling he utterly despised.

So Elden's dislike of Nate King mounted. Once he'd almost mustered the courage to fire, when they were hidden in a thicket with King kneeling in front of him. It would have been the work of an instant to lift the flintlock, touch the end of the barrel to King's head, and put a lead ball into the mountain man's brain. But Elden had hesitated, afraid of the frontiersman's cat-like reflexes. Seconds later, Nate had shifted position so they were side by side, ruining the chance.

Now, as Elden tramped along in King's wake through a tract of scattered spruce, he dejectedly hung his head and lamented the quirks of fate that had brought him to the horrible mountains. If the blackmail scheme had not gone sour, if Bascomb had not been such a jackass and followed him after dropping off the money, if Selena hadn't had to kill the fool—there were so many things that had gone wrong there at the end, it was as if they had been jinxed. Or perhaps the odds had finally caught up with them, he conceded. Sooner or later someone had been bound to suspect that Selena was his sister.

The blast of a rifle startled Elden so badly he nearly dropped his own gun. Looking up, he was flabbergasted to see a bleeding buck go leaping off into the brush.

"Come on!" Nate yelled, and raced in pursuit.

Momentarily forgetting about his plan to slay the trapper, Elden broke into a stumbling run. His heart beat with excitement at the likelihood of getting fresh meat. He was caught up in the thrill of the hunt, of seeing their hours of hard work rewarded, and he wanted to be there, to be in on the kill, so he could boast to his patronizing sister, so he could show her he was more capable than she believed. The brush snagged his clothes and limbs tried to gouge out his eyes. He slipped often on the treacherous snow and his lungs ached from the exertion. Yet somehow he kept Nate King in sight. When he saw Nate stop at the base of a steep slope, he jogged to the spot expecting to see the fallen buck. Instead, there were only tracks, leading upward. "Did it get away?" he asked anxiously.

"Not yet," Nate replied, gazing at the mountain above them. "But it has a lot more life left than I counted on." He rested the stock of his Hawken on the ground, uncapped his powder horn, and went on in disgust. "That's what happens when a shot is rushed. I took aim too fast."

"Can we catch it?"

"We can try," Nate said, pointing at red drops paralleling the tracks. "Are you up to a little climb?"

Elden leaned back to survey the full sweep of the jagged peak. The lower slopes were covered with trees and boulders, as usual, while mounds of wind-tossed snow gave the upper slopes the appearance of white sand dunes. "I'm not about to quit when we're so close," he declared.

"Good," Nate stated. He clapped Leonard on the back, then reloaded the rifle.

A grin of companionship lit up Elden's features. He hefted his rifle, eager to continue. For a few seconds he felt genuine friendship for the big trapper, and he imagined them walking into the cabin together, happily dragging the dead buck behind them. The thought made him blink, for it reminded him of what he had to do, reminded him of who he was and why he must murder one more time. A fleeting twinge of guilt assailed him, no more than a pinprick of conscience, which he dismissed with a shrug and the thought that unless he eliminated the Kings, he might swing on the gallows.

"Watch your step," Nate cautioned, taking the lead once more. Rather than forge straight up the slick incline, he climbed at a slant, crisscrossing back and forth, knowing exactly where to place his moccasins to keep from falling.

Elden was alert for the occasion he needed. Soon they were among thickly clustered trees and boulders, where no one could see them from below. They were far enough from the cabin that Elden was positive a shot wouldn't be heard. His thumb was glued to the hammer, his body tensed for the act.

The wounded buck had fled in a panic. Goaded by pain, it had made no attempt to conceal its trail as it wound haphazardly higher, passing a dozen adequate hiding places.

"Won't be long now," Nate announced, crouched to examine the snow. "It's tiring rapidly."

Elden absently nodded. He saw the trees part, and they stepped out onto a shelf heaped high with drifts. The deer had plowed on through, creating a path for them. His elbow brushed the side as he negotiated a sharp turn to the left. His attention on his footing, he failed to realize the frontiersman had stopped until his nose was almost touching King's shoulder blade. "What's wrong?"

"Take a gander," Nate said.

Easing alongside the trapper, Elden was amazed to see a sheer drop-off of 50 or 60 feet. At the bottom of the cliff lay the black-tailed buck, its head twisted at an unnatural angle, the bones in two of its shattered legs showing. "How will we get down there?" he asked.

"I don't think we can from here," Nate replied. He inched to the very edge and leaned out to better study the cliff face and the flanking slopes. To the right of the shelf the mountain seemed less formidable than elsewhere. "But we might be able to over there," he said, turning.

And Elden hit him. Taking a short step, Elden swung the flintlock in a vicious arc with all the might in his pudgy shoulders. The barrel caught Nate flush on the temple, staggering him so badly he dropped the Hawken. Closing in, Elden swung again, and again. Blood spurted. Nate sagged, doubling over, his right hand clawing at a pistol. "No, you don't!" Elden hissed, lowering the flintlock and ramming it into the trapper's chest.

Nate was hurled rearward. His legs shot over the rim. Arms swinging wildly, his face covered with crimson, he plummeted. Never once did he cry out.

Elden couldn't bear to witness the impact. Whirling, he shut his eyes and shuddered on hearing a dull thud. He waited for a yell, a wail, a moan, for anything that would tell him the mountain man had lived, but the only sound was the wind ruffling the snow. Stroking his courage, he dared peek over the edge and was bewildered on seeing no sign of King initially. Then he noticed a pair of feet jutting from a bank. He watched them for the longest while, the flintlock tucked to his shoulder, ready to fire if there was movement. But there was none.

"Well," Elden said at length. "That's that." Shouldering the rifle, he headed back down the mountain, whistling softly as he sauntered along. Selena would be pleased, he reflected. Now all they had to do was attend to the squaw, the boy, and the baby, and the cabin was theirs for as long as they needed it. He shouldn't have been so upset earlier. The day had turned out just fine after all.

Miles distant, Selena Leonard was steps away from plunging the knife into the unprotected back of Winona King when the Shoshone woman stopped and began to turn. Not caring to be caught in the act, Selena halted and swung her arm around behind her thigh, hiding the glittering blade.

"I can do the rest by myself," Winona declared, placing a large, stiff rabbit, the only animal they had removed so far from her string of snares, on top of a flat boulder. "There is no need for you to go any farther. I will leave this here and hurry back as soon as I have checked the last two."

"Nonsense," Selena said. "I wouldn't think of letting you do the work yourself." She snatched up the rabbit by its rear legs and said, "Lead the way. I've come this far. I might as well finish with you."

"As you wish," Winona said, smiling. Holding the flintlock in the crook of an elbow, she resumed heading into the gorge, her focus on the rabbit run that led back along its winding course.

A smile of a different sort twisted Selena's mouth. She dangled the dead rabbit in her left hand in front of her waist, then brought her right hand next to it so the body of the rabbit screened the knife from Winona. Moving swiftly, she caught up and coiled her right arm for the deadly thrust. As she did, she happened to notice the massive amount of snow balanced on top of the gorge wall and she remembered the avalanche Nate had caused to shake off the Bloods. Selena hesitated, deterred by the thought of the calamity that would occur should Winona scream before expiring. A single loud noise might bring all the snow crashing down.

Annoyed, Selena shoved the knife back into her pocket. She impatiently cooled her urge to kill as they went up an offshoot of the main gorge to where a snare had been set in a small stand of saplings. It was empty. The last snare, however, positioned at the end of the gorge where it widened out into a nearly frozen spring surrounded by brush and a few trees, contained another strangled rabbit.

"We have done well," Winona commented as they retraced their footsteps. "Two in one day is unusual. You have brought good medicine with you." She chuckled. "Wait until my husband sees. These are the first rabbits we have added to the pot in weeks."

"I'm glad I proved lucky for you," Selena said with undue gaiety. She was growing increasingly eager to end the charade the nearer they drew to the mouth of the gorge. Once in the clear, there would be no reason to restrain herself. Slipping her right hand into her pocket again, she affectionately caressed the bone hilt before pulling the knife and holding it against the rabbit.

"We should have a feast tonight," Winona was saying. "I will make a stew of the rabbits, and if the men have shot a deer, we can have roast venison as well."

"Sounds delicious," Selena said, increasing her pace until she was a single stride behind. A tingle of anticipation ran down her spine.

"Perhaps we can persuade my husband to sing for us," Winona chatted on. "He has a fine singing voice but he seldom uses it." She glanced back and smiled at Selena. "His parents made him join the church choir when he was young. Once a week he sang whether he wanted to or not."

"I can't wait to hear him."

Winona went around a boulder. Ahead lay the gorge entrance. "He has told me much about churches," she said, clearly delighted to have someone to talk with. "I had a hard time understanding the idea at first. My people have always believed we can worship the Great Mystery anywhere and any time. It was strange to hear that white people go to a certain lodge once a week to do so."

"There's a reason for the difference," Selena commented, her whole body vibrant with blood lust. Always was it the same. She had killed six times in her life, and each time had been an incredible experience she would never forget: the pounding of her heart, the racing of her blood, the enhancement of all her senses, the feeling of being so totally, lusciously *alive!* Now was no exception. She couldn't wait to strike, to feel Winona's warm blood gush out onto her hands.

"What is it?" Winona had responded, and slowed, for she had reached the open space fronting the gorge.

"The reason should be obvious, my dear," Selena said. Since she no longer had cause to hide her true sentiments, her tone was venomous. "Savages like you and the rest of your miserable, foul people know nothing about God, nothing about the right way to worship. All you heathens are alike. You're no better than a pack of ignorant, smelly animals and you deserve to be wiped out, every last one of you."

Winona stopped short and started to turn. "How can you say such a—?"

Selena Leonard pounced. Eyes agleam, her face a mask of devilish intent, she whipped the knife on high and rammed it into Winona's chest. The blade pierced the buffalo robe and sliced into soft flesh. Winona grunted, gasped, and tried to back up and bring her rifle to bear. Selena, however, had the advantage of surprise and speed; she batted the barrel aside and stabbed again, aiming at Winona's throat this time. Selena felt the blade cut into the robe but was uncertain whether she had drawn blood. Winona tripped, stumbled, then fell, and as she did Selena tore the flintlock loose. Stepping to one side, Selena grasped the barrel tight, swung the stock behind her, and when Winona tried to sit up, Selena smashed the stock against Winona's head. The Shoshone crumpled.

Selena dropped the rifle and stepped in close to finish the job with the knife. With Winona unconscious, she could carve and cut to her heart's content. Smiling at her victory, breathing heavily in excitement, she squatted and reached for Winona's hair so she could lift Winona's head and slit her victim's exposed throat. Her fingers were entwining in the long raven tresses when an ominous sound came from the brush to her left.

Something growled.

Releasing Winona, Selena stood and pivoted. She spotted a four-legged shape creeping stealthily through the undergrowth toward her, and thinking she was about to be charged by a wild beast, she tossed down the knife and retrieved the rifle. Fortunately, snow hadn't fouled the barrel. She cocked the piece and waited, unwilling to fire unless she was absolutely certain she could hit the animal, since if she missed it might be on her in a flash.

Again the creature growled, longer and lower this time.

There was a peculiar familiarity to the nerve-wracking challenge that Selena found puzzling. She saw the beast slink to one side into deeper brush even closer to where she stood. Suddenly, as she glimpsed its silhouette, recognition made her recoil in fright.

The creature stalking her was the Kings' tame wolf!

Selena remembered the incident that morning, and recalled her fear when the beast had behaved as if it was

going to pounce. Wolves terrified her, and rightfully so.
When she was growing up in New York, there had still
been a few wolves left in the region, and many a time
her parents or her grandparents had told her gory tales
of supposed wolf attacks during the early days of the
state. Consequently, she regarded wolves as fierceness
incarnate. They were one of the few creatures she was
truly afraid of.

The wolf stopped approximately 20 feet away, its
body poised close to the ground.

Rare indecision afflicted Selena. Her natural impulse
was to shoot, but logic dictated she save the lead ball.
She glanced at Winona, who lay as still as death, then
suddenly dropped down beside her so she could remove
Winona's ammo pouch and powder horn. No sooner did
she touch Winona, though, than the wolf uttered a ferocious snarl and glided forward.

Selena jerked upright and took swift aim. The wolf
halted a few feet shy of the edge of the brush, showing
by its caution in not stepping into the open that it had
learned through its association with the Kings exactly
what a gun could do. "Damn you!" she hissed.

The wolf stepped behind a small pine.

"Come out here, you mangy bastard!" Selena shouted,
hoping she could provoke it into a reckless act. Crouching, she stared at the pine, expecting the wolf to reappear
momentarily, but minutes went by and she saw no trace
of the thing. Her apprehension mounted. What if it was
circling her? What if it intended to get behind her, then
charge? She envisioned its iron jaws crunching down on
her bones and shivered.

A twig snapped off to the right. Selena whirled so
abruptly she nearly pitched onto her face. Recovering,
she scoured the snow-shrouded vegetation but failed to
spot movement. "Where the hell are you?" she demanded,

and was mocked by the silence of the forest.

Several more tense minutes went by. Selena tired of the wait. She saw no purpose to staying there longer. Winona hadn't budged, and as near as Selena could tell, wasn't even breathing. Although Selena preferred to stab Winona a few more times for good measure, she dreaded being set upon by the wolf if she laid another finger on the squaw. So she decided to compromise. She would leave, find Elden, and return in a short while to send Winona King on to meet her ancestors. By then the wolf might be gone. If not, Elden and her would put the thing in its place—permanently.

Retreating eastward, Selena hiked around the brush in which the wolf had first appeared, and once she was far enough off to feel safe, she headed for the cabin with all possible dispatch. Halfway there she realized she had left the dead rabbits behind, but she wasn't overly worried about obtaining food now that she knew where to find the snares Winona had set and how to set them herself.

The heavy snow tired Selena quickly. She slowed to a brisk walk, pausing every so often to catch her breath. Although she was not a good judge of distance, she guessed she was drawing near to the cabin and should spot it at any moment. Instead, as she stepped past a wide pine, she saw the north shore of the lake not 50 feet off, and figured she had overshot the cabin by a few hundred feet.

Turning to compensate, Selena spied a pair of horses moving along the east shore. She was all set to seek cover when she noticed only one rider: Her brother. With a throaty laugh, Selena ran into the open and waved her arms overhead. Elden veered around the end of the lake and galloped up in a spray of snow, his smirk telling her more than mere words could. "Where's King?" she asked anyway.

"Where do you think?" Elden retorted smugly. "Now all we have to do is take care of the bitch."

"Already done, love," Selena informed him.

"The cabin is ours, then!"

"Except for the boy and the baby."

"They're next!" Elden declared, and slid down.

Selena laughed, he laughed, and they embraced. Cackling merrily, they danced round and round like two children frolicking in the snow. They eventually stopped and stood leaning against one another, chuckling and wheezing.

"How sweet life can be!" Elden said. He puffed out his chest and smoothed his hair. "You should have seen the look on that stupid trapper's face when I sent him off a cliff! And the sound he made when he hit! Oh, it was glorious!"

"I used a knife on the squaw," Selena informed him. "But we need to go back and make sure she's dead."

"Why?"

In brief, Selena detailed how she had stabbed Winona and the subsequent intervention of the wolf, concluding with, "If I knew how to skin an animal, I'd make a rug out of the son of a bitch."

"We'll take care of it in a while," Elden said, stepping to his horse. "For now, I vote we pay the cabin a visit and tend to the King brats."

"They should be easy," Selena predicted, moving to the stallion. It shied as she grabbed the reins, but by speaking softly she was able calm the horse enough to enable her to mount.

"Everything has worked out just as we had hoped," Elden said contentedly as they rode to the trail linking the lake to the homestead. "Now we can hide here until all the snow is gone, then head for the Oregon Territory. By next fall we'll have our own place in the Willamette or Multnomah Valleys."

"Where no one knows us," Selena said with a snicker. "I'll find a rich old fur trader, someone with more money than brains, and in no time at all we'll be set up for life."

Elden glanced sharply at her. "Must we?"

"Don't start. We've been over this issue again and again. I'm tired of arguing with you."

"Then listen to reason. I don't like the idea, not one bit. Why tempt a rope? We'll have a clean slate in Oregon. We can begin new lives, decent, upstanding lives where we won't have to keep an eye over our shoulder all the time. Maybe we can open a store, or go into some other kind of business."

"How, may I ask? Without money we can't do a damn thing. Your dreams are nice, brother, but that's all they are. Flights of fancy."

"Sometimes I think you won't quit until you're three feet under," Elden said petulantly.

"Which won't happen until I'm old and wrinkled," Selena responded. "I've kept us one step ahead of the law for eight years now, haven't I? You're just jealous because you can't stand the thought of other men putting their hands on me." She shook her head in amusement. "Trust me. Everything will go smoothly as long as you rely on my judgment." Grinning, she faced westward, and was stunned to behold Zachary King standing in front of the cabin. She raised an arm to wave to him, but he suddenly whirled, ran inside, and slammed the door.

Chapter Eleven

Zachary King was mature for his years, a result of having to deal with life's often grim realities from an early age. Unlike many of his counterparts back in the States, who all too frequently were sheltered by unwise parents from the very experiences that transformed children into mature adults, he had seen rampant violence firsthand. He had witnessed death, many deaths, in fact, and observed tribal warfare. One of the initial and most important lessons he had learned was that men often killed other men. Indians, whites, it made no matter; they would slay their fellows with outright glee if the provocation was sufficient.

As a result of this fundamental education, Zachary had learned not to blindly trust strangers. His pa had repeatedly told him, "Let others earn your friendship, son, by showing they're worthy of it." And Zachary, who hung on his father's every word, did as he had been instructed.

Elden and Selena Leonard were examples of this. While Zachary thought that Selena was beautiful, he had not opened up to her because at times she had seemed rather cold, rather distant. Elden had been friendly, but almost a bit too friendly, especially after Elden had referred to him as an "Indian brat," a slight Zach had not quite forgotten. For these reasons the boy had been unable to fully open up to either of them; neither had yet earned his trust.

So now, on this sunny winter morning, when Zach stepped outside to look around for Blaze and instead spotted the brother and sister riding toward the cabin, not only was he quite surprised to find them returning without his parents, he was also perplexed to see them together when they had left separately, and on the horses, no less. His first thought was that something had happened to one or both of his folks. But if that was the case, he mused, why were Elden and Selena in such fine spirits? If there had been an accident, the pair should have raced up to the cabin in alarm. Yet there they were, taking their sweet time and chatting back and forth.

Zachary was about to hail them, to ask about his parents' well-being, when some of their words reached his ears: "three feet under" and "one step ahead of the law for eight years now, haven't I?" He saw Selena look his way, saw the shock on her face, and without being consciously aware of why he was doing so other than a feeling that something was terribly wrong, he bolted inside, shut the door, and threw the bar in place.

Outside hoofs drummed on the earth. A fist pounded on the door, and Elden Leonard called out, "Zach? What's wrong? Why have you locked us out?"

"Where are my folks?" Zach demanded suspiciously.

There was a pause, and muted, hurried whispering. Elden coughed a few times, then replied casually, "Where do you think they are? Your dad shot a deer and they're butchering it. They sent us back to fetch you and your sister."

The explanation seemed logical to Zach. He was aware of how inept the pair were. Neither knew how to track or hunt or skin game. Grinning at his foolishness, Zach stepped to the door and gripped the bar. As he did, from the other side of the door came a distinct metallic click, such as would be made when a rifle hammer was being pulled back. He hesitated, wondering why either of them would cock a gun.

"Did you hear me, boy?" Elden said. "What are you doing in there? Your parents are waiting."

Still Zach hesitated, racked by uncertainty. So many little things just didn't add up right. Yet he had no solid cause to doubt them. He had about decided he was making an idiot of himself when he heard Elden mutter two words.

"Damn brat!"

"Quiet!" Selena whispered. "He might hear you."

"I don't care," Elden snapped. "I'm cold and I'm hungry and I'm tired. If he hasn't opened this stinking door in thirty seconds, I'm kicking it in."

All of Zachary's suspicions suddenly crystallized into a dreadful certainty. He grabbed his rifle, took a step back, and leveled the barrel at the door. "I wouldn't do that if I was you," he announced. "My pa built this door to keep out bears."

"Open it!" Elden commanded.

"Not until my folks show up," Zachary said.

Elden began to angrily respond, but his statement was abruptly smothered off, as if a hand had been clamped over his mouth.

Pressing an ear to the wood, Zach listened intently. He detected bitter murmuring and suspected the brother and sister were having a quarrel. It ended quickly, at which point Selena voiced his name in a husky manner.

"I can't understand why you are behaving this way. Your father and mother will be very disappointed. Please let me in so we can discuss whatever is upsetting you."

"Go get my pa or my ma," Zach said defiantly.

"Of course, if that's what you want. But why interrupt them when they're so busy working on the deer? Doesn't it make more sense to go see them yourself?" Selena paused, apparently waiting for an answer. When none was forthcoming, she said, "Zachary, I gave you more credit than this. You're behaving rudely, even childishly. Be a good young man and kindly open the door this instant."

"I will not."

"You'll get in trouble with your parents."

"It won't be the first time."

"I'd hate to be in your shoes when your father gets ahold of you," Selena stated.

"Go get him."

"I will."

The quiet outside belied her words. Zach waited to hear hoofbeats, but there were none. He glanced at his tiny sister, peacefully sleeping on the middle of the bed, then back at the door, and as he did he glimpsed a shadow flit across the window. Crouching, he darted to the wall under the sill and warily peered out the narrow space between the leather flap and the jamb. The stallion's head was visible, nothing else.

The next instant a tremendous crash rocked the cabin as a heavy object rammed into the door, rattling the heavy bar but otherwise doing no damage.

Shifting, Zach covered the entrance. Evelyn stirred and whined, yet amazingly didn't wake up. That shortly changed when the door was again assaulted so hard the brackets holding the bar nearly popped off. Startled from her sleep, Evelyn let loose with a high-pitched cry.

"Hush!" Zach said sternly, although it did little good. He attempted to hear what was going on outdoors, and was foiled by the thick walls and his sister's wailing. Moving closer to the door, he inadvertently recoiled when yet another devastating blow shook the structure. Judging by the sound, Zach guessed that Elden was using a large log to batter the barrier. Perhaps both Leonards were involved. He had to convince them to stop before the wood shattered, and he could think of only one means of doing so. Training the flintlock on a spot to the left of the latch, he held himself still until the door was struck a third time, then he rapidly cocked and squeezed the trigger, shooting right through the wood.

A startled yelp was the reaction. A loud thud was next, and Elden screamed in outrage: "The bastard shot me! Right in the arm!"

Zach reached the window in time to observe the brother and sister disappear in the trees to the east. Moving the flap a few inches, he spied a five-foot log lying in the snow just outside the door where they had dropped it.

Evelyn, frightened badly as she had been by the fearsome din, continued to cry pathetically.

"There, there, sis," Zach said, going over. "Everything will be fine." He stroked her cheek, wishing he felt as confident as he sounded. That a terrible fate had befallen his parents was now certain, and he pondered the frightful possibility both were dead. It was as plain as the nose on his face that the Leonards intended doing the same to Evelyn and him. But why? he asked himself. What had they done to deserve this?

Seated there on the bed, Zach fought off a dark wave of despair. He must, he noted, keep his wits about him. His pa had always taught him to face hardship head-on, to tackle any job that needed doing with all his heart and soul and mind and strength, to do that job to the best of his ability. "Be a fighter, son," Nate had said. "Work hard at what you need to do. Don't give up just because something might seem impossible. It's the hard work that brings out the best in you."

Spurred by the memory, Zachary stood and took stock of the situation. There were two enemies outside who were going to try their utmost to gain entry, and there were only two ways of doing so, through the door or the window. The door was sturdy enough to withstand an hour of steady battering, as the Leonards must know by now. Which meant they would try to get in through the window.

Setting down the rifle, Zach gently picked up his sister and lowered her, blankets and all, to the floor, where he carefully slid her under the bed, out of the way of stray balls. Then, standing, he swiftly reloaded his flintlock, a task he realized he should have done sooner.

Next Zach dragged the table to a spot directly under the window and piled all the chairs on top. As he set the last one in position, a scraping noise lured him to the door. Running over, he saw the latch wiggle. Someone was trying to force it! He pointed the rifle but froze with his thumb on the hammer. Maybe that was what they wanted him to do, he reasoned. The moment he fired, the moment his gun was empty, the other Leonard would try getting in by the window.

As if to confirm his hunch, Zach spotted another shadow pass across the pane. Only this shadow didn't keep on going or vanish. It became larger, ever larger, until suddenly the entire window was blackened from top to bottom. This lasted several heartbeats. Sunshine burst into the cabin at the selfsame second the glass burst inward, smashed by a hurled log, the same one that had been employed on the door earlier. Razor shards showered all over the table and the floor, and the leather curtain was torn off and flapped downward.

Zach spun, swinging the flintlock. A bulky form blocked out the light, and there was Elden Leonard perched on the sill. Leonard tried to jump down onto the table, but the log, which lay across the sill, and the stacked chairs combined to prevent him from doing so.

Thwarted, Elden gave up trying to break inside. In his left hand he clutched a rifle, which he now tried to bring to bear.

Zach was quicker. Too quick, since his rushed shot smacked into the jamb near Elden's fingers instead of hitting Elden's shoulder. A flying wood chip must have sliced into the man's hand because Elden cried out, let go of the sill, and toppled backward.

Swift strides brought Zach to the window in time to catch sight of Elden scurrying around the northwest corner. He leaned out, eager for a shot, forgetting about Selena, a mistake he paid for when rigid claws dug into his hair and he was viciously yanked partway over the sill.

"Defy us, you little bastard!" she hissed. "I'll cut off your manhood with my own two hands!"

Zach tried to pull free; she had better leverage. He lanced an elbow backward, hoping to hit her in the stomach, but only fanned air. In desperation he reached behind him and seized her hand. She resisted him easily, laughing all the while as she continued to pull him bit by bit out of the cabin. To stop her he must release his rifle, which he was reluctant to do.

Around the corner came Elden Leonard, his features set in an arrogant sneer. He had his flintlock, and raising it, he took confident aim.

The end was seconds away. Zach couldn't hope to tear loose from Selena by relying on his strength alone before Elden fired. So acting impulsively, he dropped his rifle, drew his butcher knife, and dived. Not back in, but outward, adding his weight and momentum to the force of Selena's pull, in effect catapulting himself out the window at her very feet. She doubled over, trying to retain her hold, and their faces nearly touched.

Zach struck. With the speed of a striking ferret, he slashed his knife at Selena's throat, and had her hand not slipped from his hair, causing her to stumble backwards, he would have opened her neck wide. At it was, the blade did slit the skin, and Selena hurled herself from him, her eyes wide in shock.

"He cut me!"

Elden went rigid on seeing the blood flow down her throat. His mouth worked like that of a fish out of water. Then, recovering, he shrieked in rage and ran forward.

Shoving off the ground with his left hand, Zach leaped upward. Elden's rifle roared, lead tore into the cabin, and Zach sailed over the windowsill onto the table, colliding with the chairs he had stacked. Some crashed over the side. So did Zach. Landing on his right shoulder, he rolled against the wall and seized hold of his discarded flintlock.

Hysterical screams, fainter by the moment, pierced the air.

Taking no needless risks, Zach rose, his back to the wall, and glanced out. The Leonards were gone again, their trail easy to spot thanks not only to their tracks in the snow but also to the drops of fresh blood leading into the pines to the northeast.

For the time being, at least, Zach was safe. He sighed in relief and sank to his knees. From under the bed bubbled playful cooing and gurgling, soothing any fears he had about Evelyn.

What would the Leonards try next? That was uppermost in Zach's mind. Selena would be after him with a vengeance, so whatever they tried was bound to be swift and deadly. He could expect no mercy whatsoever.

Keeping low, Zach went to the counter and checked the bucket. It was two-thirds full. After transferring the water to a pot, he carried the pot to the fireplace and set it up on the tripod, over the flames.

Casting about for other ideas, Nate spied a coiled rope hanging on a peg. He took it down and proceeded to lay out a large loop on the floor next to the table. By positioning the piled chairs so there was a narrow gap at one side, he invited whoever entered to step off the table right into the loop.

These and additional arrangements Zachary King made over the next several hours as they occurred to him, as he waited for the killers to return.

"That damned urchin is mine!" Selena Leonard raged. "Do you hear me, Elden? Mine! If you touch him, I swear to God I'll kill you!"

"Will you calm down?" her brother requested. "You're too agitated to think straight."

"*Agitated!*" Selena exploded, and lowered her left hand to expose the thin red crease in her neck. "That son of a bitch nearly killed me! Another inch and I'd be as cold as this rotten lake!" So saying, she dipped the strip of material she had torn from the hem of her dress into the water and squeezed out the blood she had just wiped off.

"We'll get him. Be patient."

"Patient, hell! As soon as I stop bleeding, I'm going back up there and give that little rat a dose of his own medicine."

"And walk right into his sights?"

"We'll trick the upstart like we did before. Only this time you'll distract him by fiddling at the door and I'll sneak to the window," Selena proposed, grimacing as she dabbed the wound.

"He's not stupid, dear. The same ruse won't work twice."

"What do you suggest we do then?" Selena barked. "Stay out here and slowly freeze to death?"

"Nothing so drastic," Elden stated, taking a seat on a nearby log. "All we have to do is wait until dark. He won't be able to shoot what he can't see, and it should be simplicity itself for us to get close enough to pick him off."

"Except for one minor detail."

"Which is?"

"If he can't see us, we can't see him. Unless you expect him to be dumb enough to let the fire go on burning." Selena scowled in disgust. "For someone who likes to use all the big words you do, you never have been worth a damn at planning. At strategy, as you'd call it." She touched the cloth to the cut. "If it wasn't for me you would have been filling a coffin years ago."

"I know you're extremely upset over the boy, but that isn't adequate justification for venting your frustrations on me," Elden responded testily. "I've contributed my fair share to our enterprise."

"But I was the one who took most of the risks," Selena countered. "I was the one who went out in public with those men, who let myself be seen with them. What if someone who knew them had seen me and later report-ed my description to the authorities?"

"And what if one of our victims had been smart enough to have lawmen waiting at the delivery points?" Elden refused to be cowed. "Don't talk to me of risks! I took as many as you did."

Selena dipped the material into the water again, the corners of her mouth twitching downward. "At least you didn't have to go to bed with men old enough to be your father."

"Please don't remind me."

"What's wrong? I thought you had it as hard as I did," Selena shot back. "Never forget, little brother, that *I* was the one who duped those fools into liking me. I was the candy for their sweet tooths, the one who entangled them in adultery. Your part in our fine scheme, the actual blackmailing, was easy by comparison."

"Perhaps in that respect you're right," Elden conceded, his face flushing pink. "Frankly, I never have understood how you could allow others to put their hands on you, to stroke you, to do—"

"Enough!"

Elden abruptly fell silent and gazed off at the cabin, barely visible through the trees. "Agreed. Let's never bring up New York City again. Right now we have a more crucial problem, namely how to dispose of the brat and his sister so we can take possession of the cabin." He rested his rifle across his legs. "I still think we'll be able to kill him handily once the sun goes down. He's only a kid. He's bound to make a mistake."

"You had better be right," Selena said. Standing, she moved to the horses. "Mount up."

"Where are we going?"

"Back." Pressing a hand to her throat, Selena climbed into the stirrups. "Unless you want the boy to sneak off with his sister. If you'll recall, the Kings kindly revealed they have friends living north of here. The McNairs, I think they're called. If the boy should reach them, we'll have every trapper in these mountains down on our heads."

Sighing deeply, Elden stood and walked to his horse. "All this activity is sorely vexing. I'm about worn out."

"Be careful, darling," Selena said, at last relaxing enough to crack a grin. "The next thing you know, you'll grow a muscle."

Twilight gripped the Rockies when Zachary King detected a hint of movement in the forest bordering the homestead. He was crouched at a corner of the window, the rifle and a loaded pistol at his side, a knife and a tomahawk under his belt. Quickly he turned, dashed to the fireplace, and using a cup of water sparingly, extinguished the last of the embers, plunging the interior into inky darkness.

Evelyn whined and stirred in her sanctuary under the bed. She was hungry, had been for quite a while. With each passing minute she became increasingly fussier.

Zach was unable to help her even had he been free to do so. There was no milk in the cabin, nothing at all to feed her. Denied the nourishment their mother supplied, the baby would slowly starve. He shut the thought from his mind and hastened to the window.

Night was swooping down on the mountains like a great black bird of prey. Already the lake resembled a bottomless pit. The pines had changed color from green to ebony. Distant peaks, once a brilliant white, were now a ghostly gray.

Doubt set in. Zach debated for the dozenth time whether he should have tried to escape, to reach Shakespeare McNair's. He'd wanted to, even plotted how to do it, but at the moment of truth he had balked, fearing for the baby's safety in the icy wasteland he must cover.

Again something moved in the woods. Zach tried to pinpoint it without success. He tucked the pistol under his belt next to his tomahawk, then propped the rifle barrel on the windowsill and molded the stock to his shoulder. The way he figured, Elden and Selena would come at him so fast he would barely have time to think, which was just how they wanted it.

Zach heard Evelyn crying softly. Filled with concern, he shifted to stare at the bed, longing for his mother so intensely his eyes brimmed with moisture. He opened his mouth to speak to the baby, to tell it everything would be fine. Then he stiffened. Footsteps thudded on the earth right outside the window, and he heard the rustle of clothing.

Appalled that he had let his guard down, Zach faced front, saw a flitting figure, and snapped off a shot. Before he could determine if he had hit his target, the rifle barrel was seized and torn from his grasp. Backing away, he grabbed for his pistol, but in his haste he forgot about the pot of scalding water he had left on the floor. His left foot made contact. Down he went.

A deafening crash drowned out Evelyn as the chairs were sent toppling to the floor. One slammed into Zach as he was rising, throwing him off balance. He lost sight of the rope and the knives he had set out. Panicking, he drew the pistol and turned toward the table. Too late he saw a streaking form almost upon him. A knee drove into his chest with stunning force, driving him onto his back, the air whooshing from his chest. Sinewy fingers snatched his wrist and shook his right arm until the pistol flew off. Feebly he resisted, unable to accept that he had been beaten so completely, so rapidly. "No!" he cried, swinging punches that had no effect.

Chapter Twelve

A gnawing pain in Winona King's chest was the first sensation she became aware of as consciousness sluggishly returned. The second was of excruciating throbbing in her temple. Third was a sore spot on her neck. And last, but by far the oddest, was the rubbing of a soft clammy object across her face.

Belatedly, in a rush of horror, the mental images of being attacked caused Winona to open her eyes and fling her arms out to ward off more blows. But instead of seeing the demented features of Selena Leonard, she saw the somewhat sad countenance of a great wolf sporting a white mark on its chest. "Blaze?" she said softly, and was licked on the face again.

Propping an elbow on the ground, Winona weakly pushed up. The wolf whimpered and nudged her with its moist nose. "Where did you come from?" she absently asked while looking down at herself. The large bloody stain on her dress made her shiver as she recalled being stabbed close to the heart and in the neck.

In the final, terrifying moments of Selena's unexpected onslaught, Winona had believed she was going to die, and she could hardly believe she had been miraculously spared. Gingerly, she eased out of her robe. By touching her neck she discovered the tip of the knife had merely nicked her throat; the thick robe had saved her from more severe injury. But what about the stab wound in the chest? Her fingers trembling, heedless of the biting wind, Winona lowered the top of her dress as she had done to feed the baby.

The knife had been aimed directly at her heart. Had she not been turning as the blow was delivered, and had the blade not been partially deflected by the heavy folds of her robe, she would had died on the spot. But the knife had penetrated at an angle above her left breast, slicing deep into the flesh but missing her heart and sparing her life.

Winona bowed her head in silent gratitude. When Blaze nudged her again, she looked up and scratched the wolf under the chin. "Where did the white woman go?" she wondered, grimacing as the throbbing in her temple combined with the pain in her chest to nearly make her pass out.

Suddenly Winona's torment was utterly forgotten. With a start she realized there was only one logical place the woman would have gone: the cabin. "My baby!" Winona cried. "My son!" Curling her legs under her, she rose unsteadily. Dizziness assailed her, and she took a few disjointed, stumbling steps. She feared she would collapse, but the dizziness subsided as abruptly as it had flared.

"Evelyn," Winona said, aghast, beset by appalling visions of the infant receiving the same savage treatment she had received. Turning, she glanced at the sky to get her bearings. She was shocked to see the sun half gone, twilight about to descend. It meant she had been unconscious all afternoon! It meant Selena had had plenty of time to . . .

Winona refused to finish the thought. Bending over, she clutched at her robe, bringing on another bout of dizziness. Her stomach churned, threatening to heave. Somehow she retrieved the robe and straightened, and once she did she immediately felt a little better. Gritting her teeth, Winona shrugged into the garment that had been her salvation. She was aware of blood trickling down her front but she refused to take the time to tend the wound, not when the lives of her offspring were at stake.

Anxiety for Nate added to Winona's alarm. She had no idea why Selena had attacked her, yet clearly the act had been premeditated. Clearly the Leonards must have had sinister designs on her entire family from the very first. Had Elden, then, jumped Nate when her husband had least expected it? She remembered the shot she had heard as she left the cabin, and her fists clenched in suppressed rage.

Winona headed homeward, taking only a few strides before she glimpsed the hilt of a knife protruding from the snow, a knife she recognized as once having belonged to her mother, the very knife she had lent Selena, the weapon, ironically, used against her by the woman. Stopping, she willed her body to bend once more so she could pick it up.

At last, knife in hand, the wolf at her side, Winona resumed walking. She was critically weak, her limbs balking at every movement, her chest in absolute torture. Yet she shuffled on. In grim determination, fired by anxiety for those she loved the most, she hiked south-eastward.

Determination, however, was no match for Nature. The loss of blood and the punishment her body had endured took their toll before she went a mile. Her legs gave out, and with a low moan she fell to her knees and swayed. "No! she said. "I will not give up!"

Blaze, standing near at hand, looked at her and whined.

Inspiration prompted Winona to beckon the animal closer. Obediently, it came, and locking the fingers of her left hand in its hairy coat above the front shoulders, she urged, "Move, boy! Help me! Move!"

Evidently sensing her design, the wolf threw its whole body forward, straining its legs to their limit, and by sheer brute strength swept Winona from her knees and to her feet. She stopped, holding the animal close, wary of pitching over if it should leave her.

"You get all the deer meat you can eat for this," Winona joked, but it brought no smile to her grimly compressed lips. The stakes were too high for levity.

Taking deep breaths, Winona firmed her muscles and gave Blaze a slight push. The wolf started off, making no attempt to break loose, casting a concerned eye at her now and again. She clung to it as a drowning person would cling to a floating branch, afraid she would go down and be unable to get up again without its help.

Once among the pines, Winona had a difficult time telling which way they should go. Ordinarily so simple a task would have posed no problem, but in her disoriented state she often became briefly confused, unable to distinguish north from south, east from west. The intermittent dizziness only made the situation worse.

So did the darkness. Once the sun sank, Winona could no longer rely on it to highlight the western horizon.

More often than not she had to guess at the direction she was traveling, and frequently she would spot a tree or boulder she knew and realize with a building sense of futility that she was going the wrong way.

Eventually, on the verge of outright collapse, Winona halted, wiped a hand across her perspiring brow, and looked to her left. She gaped in surprise at seeing the lake dozens of yards off. From the shape of the shoreline, she knew she must be somewhere between the lake and the cabin. Twisting, she nearly shouted for joy on spying the dark outline of the structure not 30 yards off.

The next instant the night reverberated to the blast of a rifle. Winona saw flame and smoke leap from the cabin window. In her befuddled state she believed she was the target. Releasing Blaze, she took a faltering stride to one side at the very second a heavy hand fell on her shoulder and she was seized around the waist from behind.

Cold. Intense, complete, cold.

Nate King had never been so utterly cold. He shivered, he shook, his teeth chattering, and tried to worm his way deeper into the warm blankets enveloping him. Oddly, the blankets were moist and clung to his skin. The wet added to his discomfort. He twisted, trying to pull the blankets tighter around his shoulders, and his fingers plunged into a mushy substance.

Bewildered, Nate blinked, came fully awake, and felt his pulse surge when he comprehended the truth: He was encased in a vault of snow, literally buried alive! Panic set in. He thrashed wildly and surged against the mass pressing on his back. His hands brushed the tops of boulders buried under him. His head began pounding. He felt a nearly irresistible urge to scream.

Suddenly the snow walls around Nate caved in. Certain he was about to be smothered alive, he flailed and kicked at the constricting white shroud. A second later he was in the clear and breathing fresh air. He sat up, snow covering him from his waist on down, and looked around in confusion. Slowly the truth dawned as he recalled being knocked off the cliff by Elden Leonard. His hand shot to his face and he felt the welts and gashes left by the beating Elden had inflicted. In his mind's eye he could see, again, the barrel of the greenhorn's rifle glinting in the sunlight as it rained down on his head. Once again he experienced the flow of air past his body and saw the white earth rushing up to meet him. By a sheer accident he had plowed into a deep drift that had spared him from being crushed on the underlying boulders.

Batting the snow aside, Nate stood. His legs were a bit shaky and his head hurt abominably, but otherwise he felt fine. He tested his arms, insuring neither was broken. Then he faced the cliff. By the position of the sun he knew he had been out for many hours. Already it was late afternoon. What had Elden been up to in all that time? he asked himself, and felt a chill at the possible answer.

"Winona and the kids!" Nate said softly. He headed for the slope to the left of the sheer precipice, the slope he had studied from above and thought might be gradual enough to be negotiated. His new perspective gave him doubts. The lower portion was quite steep, the snow bound to be as slippery as ice. Getting up there would tax him to his core, and might even prove fatal if he should slip near the top, yet he had it to do. The lives of his loved ones were at stake, and nothing was going to keep him from reaching them.

Filled with apprehension, Nate hiked to the base of the slope and paused. There were no trees nearby, which was disappointing since he could have used a limb as a crutch to help keep his footing. Shrugging at the inevitable, Nate commenced his ascent. Right away he discovered the footing was extremely treacherous, even worse than he'd expected. He had to lay each foot down just so or his sole would slide out from under him.

Climbing a mountain of ice would have been no easier. Nate gave up trying to stand after a while and simply crawled upward on all fours, digging his fingers and toes into the snow for extra purchase. When the going became particularly steep, he lay flat and wormed his way higher inch by precarious inch. Only once did he look down, when he was about halfway up, and the thought of falling again almost made him do just that. Resisting a wave of vertigo, he applied his energy to climbing. Nothing but climbing. He emptied himself of distracting thoughts and feelings. He reined in his pain.

Nate tired but never slowed. The cold was a foe to be dominated, to be conquered by the force of his will. His hands grew frigid, his fingers nearly numb. Despite this, higher and higher he climbed. Sweat poured from every pore and was promptly cooled by the wind. Fortunately, his exertions countered most of the chill.

Reach. Dig in. Lift a leg. Dig in. It was the same routine over and over and over again. Nate was like one of those steam engines he had read about, mechanically doing the same thing so many times his movements became automatic. His brain seemed to shut off. Reach. Dig in. Lift a leg. Dig in.

When Nate's hand extended and made contact with nothing but empty air, he snapped back to life and looked up to learn he was at the point where the shelf blended into the slope. Leaning to his right, he hooked an elbow on the shelf, then propelled himself forward by kicking off with both legs. He rolled once and came to a stop close to the edge.

Grinning, Nate rose on his hands and knees. His muscles cried for rest, yet he had to go on. Moving back a yard, he stood and walked toward the gap in the drifts. A long, dark shape in the snow stopped him. He buried his arm to the elbow and drew out his Hawken, left by Elden where it had fallen.

"Thank you, fool," Nate muttered. The barrel was clogged, so he swiftly tugged out the ramrod, cleaned out the snow, and reloaded. It was then he realized one of his pistols was gone, probably lying in the drift into which he had plummeted. Guns were precious, but his family was even more so. Making a note to go back for the pistol later, he hurried on down the mountain.

The climb had taken hours. Nate stared at the blood-red sun, perched above the western mountains, and goaded his weary legs into a trot. His sense of urgency mounted the further he ran. He cursed himself for being the biggest ass in all of creation, for endangering those who mattered most to him. But how was he to have known? Rescuing the Leonards had been a good deed on his part—or so he'd believed.

Running now became as mechanical as the climb had been. Nate's legs seemingly moved of their own volition. Presently the lake came into view. The surface glimmered gold with fading sunlight as he started around the east side, but darkness covered it by the time he came to the west side, within hailing distance of the cabin.

Exhaustion nipped at Nate's heels. He wanted to keel over, to sleep for a month. Angling to the lake, he knelt and splashed handfuls of the frigid water onto his face and neck. It had the desired result, temporarily reviving him, sharpening his senses. He held the Hawken in his left hand, rose, and cut into the trees on a beeline for his home. Night reigned, restricting his vision to a few dozen feet.

Nate saw someone up ahead, a blurred figure moving in the same direction he was. He detected long hair. Instantly unadulterated rage pulsed through him. He slowed, moving as silently as a wraith, his wrath building as he thought of getting his hands on Selena Leonard.

The woman was only a few feet away, hunched over as if she was sneaking toward the cabin, when several things happened all at once. Nate pounced at the very moment a rifle shot shattered the quiet of the forest and the woman straightened and moved to one side. He identified her profile as his hand closed on her shoulder. Wrapping his other arm around her waist, he whispered in her ear, "Winona! It's me!"

A streak of fur took off from her side. Nate heard her gasp, and she sagged against him. From the cabin came a terrible tumult. Selena Leonard was shouting. Suspecting that his children were in dire trouble, Nate quickly lowered Winona to the ground. He felt blood on his hand, and would have lingered had his son's fevered voice not reached his ears.

"Let go of me! Let go!"

"I'll be back!" Nate told Winona. Tearing his gaze away, he sprinted for the cabin door. A new element was added to the mayhem: the ferocious snarling and snapping of a raging wolf, attended by screams of terror and gruff masculine curses. A gun cracked. The snarling heightened to a frenzy. And through it all Zach was yelling, "Get her! Get her! Get her!"

Nate hit the door at a full run. He knew it was closed; he never expected it to be barred as well. The impact sent him flying backward, dazed and aching, onto the ground. He dimly heard a crashing noise, then the thud of frantic footsteps. Someone—or were there two of them?—rushed off into the trees.

"Zach!" Nate boomed, lurching upright. He staggered to the window, but could see little in the gloom.

"Pa? Is that you?"

"Where are you?" Nate responded, throwing a leg over the sill. The table blocked his path and was angrily hurled aside. "Are you and you sister all right?"

Nate took a step, then stopped as a thin form hurtled at him and eager arms encircled his hips. He gripped his son's arm and asked, "The Leonards, Zach? Are they gone?"

"Yes," Zach answered, the word distorted by the sob of relief that was uttered with it. "Blaze . . . Blaze did . . ." He broke off to sniffle.

"Evelyn?" Nate pressed. "Where's your sister?"

"Under the bed, Pa. She's fine."

Prying the boy's arms loose, Nate squatted and gave his son a tearful hug. Zach's whole body shook, and Nate knew the boy was trying to hold back his tears. Nate's eyes had adjusted enough to note the broken chairs and other items scattered all about. He also saw a familiar dog-like body lying on the floor. "Blaze?" he blurted out, fearing the worst.

The wolf stood and padded over to him. Its tongue flicked his wrist.

"Blaze saved me, Pa," Zach said, his voice husky with emotion. "That Selena woman was strangling the daylights out of me. I could barely breathe, and I figured I was a goner." Turning, he looped an arm over the wolf. "I was seeing spots, I was. And suddenly Blaze was there and tearing at her arms. She had to let go to save herself. Elden fired at him but missed. Next I knew, they were both running for their lives."

"They won't get away," Nate vowed. Going to the bed, he flattened on the floor, located a bundle of blankets, and pulled his daughter out.

In the forest hoofbeats sounded, bearing to the northwest and fading rapidly.

"The Leonards!" Zach cried.

"In due time," Nate said somberly as he deposited Evelyn on the bed and pried the wrap apart so he could see her beaming cherubic face. "Happy to see me, are you?" he asked, his voice as husky as his son's.

"She's awful hungry," Zach mentioned. "Where's Ma, Pa? Why isn't she here?"

"Oh, Lord," Nate breathed. Springing up, he dashed to the door and wrenched the bar loose. "Start a fire!" he directed over his shoulder. "I'll be right back."

"Do you know where Ma is?" Zach hollered.

"I'm going to fetch her," Nate answered, neglecting to add that he hoped he wasn't already too late.

Somewhere sparrows chirped. Warm sunshine bathed Winona as she opened her eyes and found her daughter cradled in the crook of her arm, sound asleep. Looking up, she beheld two of the gloomiest human beings alive. Winona grinned, watching them pick at bowls of stew on the table in front of them, and remarked, "I see your father has done the cooking again."

A pair of gleeful maniacs rushed to the bed and smothered Winona with hugs and kisses. She reveled in their affection. Once she winced when Zach accidentally bumped the bandage covering her left side. When finally they calmed down, she inquired sarcastically, "Have you missed my food that much?"

"Oh, Ma!" Zach said, laying his head on her good shoulder. "You had us worried for a spell."

"You've been out for two days," Nate added, stroking her forehead. "Had a high fever for a while too, but we got it under control."

"Our guests?"

"Rode out of here like their tails were on fire," Nate said. "I aim to track them down just as soon as you're up and about." A cloud darkened his face. "They won't ever do to anyone else what they did to us."

Winona felt Evelyn squirm. She tenderly touched the baby's cheek as a knot formed in her throat and her lungs became constricted. "God smiled on us," she said, using her husband's word for the Great Mystery.

Nate nodded, and remarked, "One good thing came out of this nightmare."

"What might that be?" Winona asked.

"You won't have to be so fussy about keeping the cabin spruced up from now on. It'll be a cold day in hell before I bring anyone home with me again."

They all laughed then, the nervous laughter of tension long denied being abruptly released, laughing harder and longer than was called for, but laughing anyway until none of them could laugh anymore.

"Visitors will always be welcome here," Winona said afterward. "We cannot judge everyone by the way the Leonards acted." She relaxed and grinned contentedly until her husband's words sank in. "Did you say I have been unconscious for two days?"

"It'll be three this evening," Nate amended.

"How have you managed to keep our tiny one fed all that time?"

"She sort of fed herself."

"How?"

Nate nodded at her bosom, then coughed and fidgeted.

"How?" Winona repeated, guessing the truth and marveling at his audacity. Usually he was extremely shy about such matters, which she understood was a typical trait of many whites.

"Well," Nate began, "your left side was hurt but your right side wasn't, so whenever Evelyn acted hungry, I tucked her in with you and let her do as she pleased."

"It was really funny, Ma," Zach interjected. "Evelyn kept flopping off of you, so Pa had to hold her in place. Last night he fell asleep while doing it, and when I woke up this morning, there was his face right where Evelyn's was supposed to be."

Winona saw a pink hue creep up her husband's features. She threw her right arm around him, pulled him close, and boldly gave him a kiss full on the lips. "Have I ever told you that I love you?"

"Every day."

"I hope you are not bored of hearing it because I will tell you the same thing each and every day until we go under."

"You can engrave it on my forehead if you want," Nate quipped, leaning down to peck her nose. As he raised up, he glanced at the remnants of a broken chair that had been stacked next to the fireplace and a flinty gleam came into his narrowed eyes.

There was no need for Winona to ask about the reason. She knew what he was thinking as surely as she knew her own thoughts, just as she knew there would be no convincing him to change his mind even had she been so inclined. So she made the only comment she could under the circumstances. "You be careful, my husband. They will not let themselves be taken alive."

"I'm counting on that," Nate said harshly, and his hand closed on the hilt of his big knife.

Chapter Thirteen

Two more days elapsed before Nate was satisfied his wife had recovered sufficiently to justify his departure. He packed a pair of parfleches with the supplies he would need, saddled a sorrel before daylight, and was on the trail by the time the sun crowned the eastern sky. Although the tracks were old, they were easy to follow since very little melting had taken place.

By mid-morning it became apparent the fleeing pair had no idea which way to go. The trail went northwest for a few miles, changed to due west, then to due north. Nate noted only one constant: Elden and Selena always took the easiest course, no matter where it led them.

When sunset painted the heavens brilliant hues of red, orange, and yellow, Nate had traveled over 20 miles, but only a dozen from his cabin as the crow flies. He could have reached the same spot in a third of the time had he been relying on his own judgment.

The next day was more of the same. And the next. The circuitous trail was so ridiculous it was maddening. Nate had hoped to be able to gauge the direction of their travel and take one of the many shortcuts he knew of to cut them off, but their insane meandering required him to stick with the trail at all times, slowing him down.

There was one consolation. At the rate they were traveling, Nate expected to overtake them late on the fourth day. He was pushing the sorrel, riding at twice the speed they were. And where they had stopped often, perhaps to take brief rests or to argue over which way to go next, he seldom halted.

That night, as Nate sat beside a crackling fire warming his hands, he wondered how the pair were managing to fill their bellies. He'd come on the remains of several of their campfires and not once seen evidence they had cooked game. Either they were living on bark and twigs, which he doubted they had the stomach for, or they were going without food. If so, they might be too weak to lift a finger against him when he caught them. And he wanted them to resist. He wanted them to put up a fight so he could slay them without regret.

Dawn found Nate in the saddle, Hawken in hand, resuming his journey. Today was the day. Excited to be so close to them, he forged ahead for several hours. Then, as he came through a pass into a spacious valley, he saw something which made him rein up sharply and curse.

Others had found the trail. Five unshod horses had approached at a walk from out of the northeast. On finding the tracks they had halted and one of their number had dismounted to better study the impressions, as shown by the moccasin prints paralleling the trail for a short distance. The man had climbed back on his mount and all five had gone on, three on one side of the tracks, two on the other.

With a jab of his heels Nate brought the sorrel to a gallop. He was furious at this latest development. Whether the Indians were friendly or hostile was irrelevant. Either would spoil his vengeance. Friendly warriors, such as those from a Shoshone village, might take the Leonards to Fort Laramie if the pair made their wants known. Hostiles, on the other hand, might kill them before he caught up.

Nate rode hard toward the end of the valley. He was still half a mile from it when he saw smoke, a slate-gray column spiraling skyward beyond a patch of pines. Veering to the left, he took advantage of all available cover until he was close enough to smell the acrid scent of burning wood. He slid down, tied the sorrel to a limb, crouched, and stalked through the underbrush. Presently he spotted men in buckskins moving in a clearing. He heard laughter and low voices.

From there on Nate exercised the caution of a panther, gliding silently from tree to tree or boulder to boulder. When he had caught enough of the tongue being spoken to recognize it, he wanted to kick something. Anything. He could hardly believe his luck. What were the odds? he kept asking himself.

The Indians were Bloods.

From behind a spruce tree Nate scanned their camp. The seven horses were tied in a row to the right. In the middle of the clearing blazed a small fire. To the left, their arms bound to saplings, their heads bowed, were Selena and Elden Leonard. In front of them stood the five braves.

Nate had no way of knowing if the warriors were part of the same bunch he had tangled with days ago, but he suspected they might well be. They were having great fun poking and slapping the Leonards, or mocking their captives with lewd gestures. Selena was being mistreated too, and it was this fact more than anything else which indicated to Nate the braves were some of those he had fought before, now out for revenge.

Warriors rarely abused white women because having a white wife was a symbol of prestige and considered good medicine. White women were often pampered, accorded better treatment than their Indian sisters. But not this time. Selena was being jabbed and struck as hard as her brother, as if out of spite.

Nate felt no sympathy at all for their plight. Any compassion he might have felt had died when the pair tried to kill his family. In his opinion they were getting exactly what they deserved. Justice was being served. His only regret was that others were doing the serving.

"Dear God! No!"

At Elden's cry, Nate glanced up and saw that a stocky warrior had drawn a knife. He watched the man step up to Elden and lightly run the blade over Elden's face, around the nose and under the chin, leaving a pencil-thin wake of blood.

Elden was too petrified to do more than gawk. But when the brave lowered the knife, Elden started crying and blubbered, "Spare me! Please! I'll do anything you want! Just don't hurt me! That's all I ask."

"Be quiet, you spineless worm!" Selena snapped. "For once try to pretend you're a real man."

"I don't want to die!" Elden wailed.

"Do you think I do?" Selena retorted. "But you don't see me behaving like a coward."

"Go to hell!" was her brother's rejoinder. He appeared ready to say more, but the stocky brave suddenly drove the bloody knife to the hilt in Elden's groin.

Nate flinched at the sight, his skin erupting in gooseflesh at the high-pitched shriek the greenhorn vented. He saw the warrior yank the knife out, saw blood pumping from the hole in Elden's pants, and averted his eyes as his stomach churned. When next he looked, Elden was babbling hysterically and struggling against his bounds like one demented.

The Bloods cackled at his antics. The louder he grew, the louder they laughed.

Having lived with and among Indians for years, Nate knew many tribes liked to torture captives. The knife in the loins was just the beginning for Elden Leonard. Before morning came, the man would be begging the warriors to finish him off, to put him out of his misery, and Nate didn't care to witness the whole ordeal. He was glad he had something else to do.

Retreating into the forest, Nate worked his way around to the horses. His stallion and mare were tied in the middle of the string. Slinking up behind them, he peered between their legs to verify the Bloods were still busy with the Leonards; then he rose beside the stallion and swiftly unfastened its reins. The same was done for the mare. With reins in each hand, Nate slowly turned the animals and hastened into the trees. Elden's screams smothered any noise he made.

Nate took the horses to where he had left the sorrel. He placed a hand on his saddle, preparing to swing up, when a wavering screech caused the sorrel to prance nervously away from him and ravens in nearby trees to take wing. Turning, he listened to the most awful cry of despair and terror he had ever heard, a cry that set his teeth on edge, that lingered on and on and finally subsided into a pathetic moan.

"It doesn't concern me," Nate said angrily. He stepped to the sorrel, started to mount, then paused. The moaning seemed like it would never end. He waited, and waited. Then, frowning, mad at himself for being so softhearted, he ground-hitched the three horses and raced back to the same spruce he had hidden behind minutes ago.

Both Elden and Selena were on the ground, spread-eagle, totally naked. Ringed around them were four of the five Bloods. The fifth was between Selena's legs. But she wasn't the one moaning. That was Elden. With excellent cause. The Bloods had amused themselves by depriving him of his manhood, slitting open his abdomen so his intestines dangled out, and chopping off his nose and ears.

Nate had seen many mutilations, had observed atrocities that would make most people sick on sight. These were no different, yet they bothered him, and in being bothered he became further upset because by all rights he should be overjoyed to see the Leonards get their comeuppance. Why did he feel the way he did?

One of the warriors changed places with the man on the ground. This one, to heighten his pleasure, hoisted Selena's legs over his shoulders.

The angle gave Nate a clear view of Selena's face. Her expression was as dead as that of a corpse, devoid of all emotion, like a blank mask sculpted from white clay. The brave's shoulders blocked her torso from sight until the man was done and stood. Then Nate discovered the tips of her breasts had been cleanly removed. Bile rose in his mouth. He lifted the Hawken, but hesitated.

Another warrior took up position, the stocky one who had cut Elden's face. The man laughed and slapped Selena's behind, trying to induce her to cooperate. Her empty eyes must have made him mad, because he drew back a fist and punched her full on the mouth. When she sagged, he barked directions at two of his fellows, who then stepped forward, each to grab her by an arm, and lifted her until she stood limply erect.

Nate knew what he was going to do before the stocky brave drew the bloody knife. He knew, and he was furious. Taking a quick look back, he plotted out the path he must follow to reach his horses as swiftly as possible. He would have a five- to ten-second head start, since it would take that long for the Bloods to realize they weren't under attack and to sprint in pursuit. That should be more than enough time. He'd be on the sorrel and hundreds of yards off before they broke into the open. When they saw him, they'd no doubt turn and race for their horses, taking another minute. By the time they broke from the trees he would be half a mile off. If they began to gain, he'd stop and drop one or two with the Hawken to discourage the rest. Then it was on to the cabin and his family.

With the details all worked out, Nate placed his cheek to the smooth stock of the Hawken and took deliberate aim. The stocky brave had swept his knife arm back so he could bury the blade in Selena.

The next instant Nate King shot her smack between the eyes.